Operation
Raven Rock

By

R.T. Breach

Operation Raven Rock by R.T. Breach

Published by Covert Publishing House
280 Merchants Dr
Unit 2921
Dallas, GA 30132

www.rtbreach.com

For permissions, contact:

rtb@rtbreach.com

Cover by CovertWebMan

Editing by Sandra Haven

ISBN: 978-1-7363786-8-7

dedIcated
to
all the
tin-foil hat
wearing people.
The truth is out there.

I

"Don't make a fuss about a world war. At most, people die. Half the population wiped out. This happened quite a few times in Chinese history. It's best if half the population remains, next best one-third."

- Mao Zedong

01:35, December 5th, 2019–Gobi Desert, Mongolia

Clandestine agents in the field have a certain amount of leeway and flexibility during operations. Being out of touch isn't unusual. Staying out of touch sets off alarm bells. American Central Intelligence Agency Officer Tonya Chi-Hye remained silent forty-eight hours past her check-in time. Techs noted the time and triangulated her last transmission. Pilots from the emergency drop days before reported seeing what appeared to be Chi-Hye and several Mossad operatives. She'd been working with them in Mongolia.

In response, the CIA dispatched a five-man paramilitary team. Aboard a blacked-out C-130, the squad of Americans prepared themselves for a sub-zero, low-altitude, night parachute insertion. As the craft neared the last known locus of Chi-Hye, an air crewman lowered the military cargo plane's aft ramp. Freezing air billowed into the red-lit fuselage and five black-clad agents, parachutes strapped on, stepped into line.

The crewman, grasping a handhold, leaned out the opening. *Man, there ain't shit out here. I'm glad it's these guys jumping and not me.* He shivered, peering over a shoulder at the readying agents. In a few minutes, they'd be gone and he could close the door.

The jumpers clasped carabiners on an overhead cable, checking gear on each other like chimps looking for lice. Agents Perkins, Fernandez, Crutchlow, Roberts, and Moreland wore black fatigues like those worn by the First People of Evolution. Perkins, having seen the terrorist organization up close with Agent Chi-Hye, recommended the outfits in case they needed to portray themselves as members of FPE.

As the senior agent, he was in charge. Not that this was his preference; he was only a month away from retiring. Here he was in the heat of action once more. The universe was trying hard to ruin his last few weeks in the CIA. It made Perkins grind his teeth every time he thought about it. All he had to do was get this mission over with and cruise on back home to the States.

Unknown to him, the FPE died in a plane crash. Mossad agent, Karl Gruben, blew up their YAK-42 jetliner mid-flight with a couple of grenades. Perkins was unaware of that drama, oblivious to Gruben's narrow escape, only to be captured. Or of how his heroic deed saved millions of people. A Bubonic plague bio-weapon got destroyed in the plane accident.

A week before now, Perkins had been with Chi-Hye's team, now lost on the dark desert floor. The Mossad team-lead, Karl Gruben, drove Perkins off the deep end with his reckless antics, until he abandoned the mission, Mossad team, and Chi-Hye in the Gobi Desert. Given an ultimatum: go with Perkins or stay, Chi-Hye had hesitated. Disgusted, Perkins split. He wasted no time returning to base. It still took two days driving alone in the desert.

The CIA, in coordination with Western Mongolian authorities, had a hidden base of operations west of Ulaanbaatar. Nestled in a canyon, with a hard packed runway suitable for C-130s and smaller aircraft, it stretched out five hundred meters along the valley floor. Worn out by the desert trek, Perkins had collapsed in bed. Six hours later, he got awakened. Tonya Chi-Hye still hadn't reported in on her status.

I knew they'd get themselves killed.

The CIA ordered him to locate her. Fearing the worst and guilt-ridden, Perkins and four other agents geared up for Operation Raven Rock. They boarded the C-130 at 00:28 hours. One hour out, they were circling Chi-Hye's last known location with the ramp down. Spiraling outward from there, they combed the dark desert. Nose mounted FLIR (Forward Looking Infra-Red) images detected a lone vehicle in short order. The jeep-like construction was surely the emergency transportation they'd air dropped days ago.

The C-130 pilot banked a wide turn, circling back to line up on the drop zone. Small, head-level red lights along the fuselage's interior flared green.

Perkins sucked in a deep breath, turned back, and made eye contact with his four comrades. He twirled a finger. "Ready?"

Four shadowy thumbs and nods replied.

He nodded and turned, facing a black maw at the extended loading ramp's foot. After another deep breath, he took two steps, then fell forward, disappearing into the night.

The rest of the team followed suit, diving into the ink beyond the ramp's edge. Icy air blasted through their clothing, setting them shivering in seconds, plummeting back to Earth. Mercifully, it was a short jump. In less than a minute, they were on the ground.

"Holy shit, that was cold!" Esteban Fernandez said, as he rapidly unfastened parachute straps. He came down by Jerry Crutchlow, a sandy-haired Caucasian. A quarter moon lit the landscape in a pale green hue. Dark smudges of scrub and rock dotted the area.

"Fucking-A it was," Crutchlow said. He was winding up his lines and chute into a wad. Peering around, an armload of parachute hugged to his chest, Crutchlow made out the other three team members' vague silhouettes twenty meters away. Lowering his voice, he said, "I see the others. Looks like we're all okay."

"Roger, that." Fernandez stepped next to Crutchlow. "Let's *vamos*." He glanced around furtively. "I think we landed east of the target."

Crutchlow nodded and hand signaled 'move out.'

The agents assembled one by one around Perkins, resolving out of the moon glow into shadows approaching. They squatted in a huddle.

Perkins asked, "Is everybody good?"

Nods all around.

Fernandez said, "Me and Crutch came down okay."

Moreland said, "I'm good."

Tate Roberts said, "I'm good. Ready to rock."

A wire ran from Perkins' earpiece to a chest pocket occupied by a radio. He keyed it. "Crow's nest, this is Raven One."

Perkins was the most experienced of them all, with almost twenty years. Crutchlow was the next senior of twelve years. Moreland and Roberts had eight years, while Fernandez was most junior at five years with the CIA.

The static hiss cut off. A female voice said, "Go ahead, Raven One."

"Raven One has landed."

"Roger that, Raven One. Be safe."

Perkins tugged out a portable GPS device from his other chest pocket. Its dim glow illuminated the faces framed by black watch caps. "Let's see... we're here. Target is there." He popped his head up a moment, then consulted the GPS compass, divining their proximity to the jeep. "Looks like we're a hundred meters from the drop zone." He stretched an arm west. "In that direction." He rose from one knee and took a few steps toward their target. "Stash your chutes and come on." Perkins stuffed his under a boulder. The others did the same, then fell in behind, spacing three or four meters apart, single file.

Perkins spied the jeep first, ten meters off. He took a knee. His team halted and kneeled. They waited a long minute. Still night air amplified Perkins' tinnitus. But no sounds of danger broke the silence. He turned to Fernandez and signaled him to go check out the jeep. Fernandez wordlessly crept forward. Upon reaching the jeep, he circled it, standing erect when he signaled the okay.

Perkins and the others jogged over, huddling near the car's hood.

"Nothing here. Fuck, I'm freezing," Fernandez said. Having grown up in Texas heat, his blood was as thin as water. Cold climates made him miserable and homesick.

A brief search of the jeep gave no clues, save multiple tire tracks, discovered by Crutchlow, heading south. They hiked briskly along the trail, trying to save time and keep warm simultaneously. Three hours later, they came upon a cluster of small vehicles. Holding fifteen meters out, the team observed the situation.

"I'm not seeing any movement," the dark-haired, quiet Roberts said. "Either they're abandoned or the owners are sleeping inside."

"Yeah," Perkins said, peering at the cars, which appeared to be mini-Coopers. "Alright, Moreland, Crutchlow, Roberts. Go see what's up."

The three agents crouched, submachine guns shouldered, and stalked toward the cars. As they neared the first, a waft of putrid odor made them grimace.

"What the fuck is that stench?" Moreland said, covering his mouth and nose. "Something's dead over here." He paused at the first car, snapped on a barrel-mounted red light and immediately turned away. "Oh, god!" Moreland backed off, holding down a dry heave.

Crutchlow got a glimpse of the three corpses riddled with bullet holes—not Mongolians, but college-aged white kids. He moved on to the next car. Light on, he and Roberts found nothing but dozens of tiny bullet holes in the other cars.

Moreland tripped and stumbled over the last corpse lying near the body-filled car. "Oh, god," He cried. "What the fuck? Dude! What the fuck?" He scrambled away toward Perkins, who was at the first car, fingering a bullet hole in its hood.

"That's a tiny caliber. Something dumped a few hundred rounds. Turned these cars and people into Swiss cheese. Are they civilians?"

Moreland, hand to his mouth, dropped it, shaking his head. "Yeah, man. Kids. They're just some fuck'n kids."

Perkins gripped Moreland's shoulder, lips pressed. "Keep watch while I check things out." He turned to the others. "You guys post up at that last car." Perkins turned back to the first car, pulling a small hand towel from around his neck, covering his mouth and nose. Eyebrows knit, he leaned in and shined a white lit flashlight around inside. The gruesome scene was the worst he ever laid eyes on. He spied a wallet clutched in dead fingers, reached in gingerly, and lifted it free. A quick rifling through the wallet's contents told him at least this one was an American. *These guys ain't players. Must've got hit by mistake or caught in some crossfire.* He spun away, glad to put the gory image behind.

"Come on. We're moving out." Moreland gladly followed.

Five shadows converged in the night.

Fernandez asked, "What do you think happened?"

Perkins shook his head. "Looks like they were in the wrong place at the wrong time. They're not operators. No weapons." He gazed into the gloom. "Just some kids in this godforsaken desert."

"I'll bet they were running in that rally race," Fernandez said with a sniff, snugging his jacket collar. "Those cars look like the right type."

Perkins peered back at the ventilated minis. "Whatever happened, those aren't our people. Looks like they got away. Crutch, you're sure there were four? Maybe they were already gone and its mistaken identity. With that Mossad guy, Gruben, who knows?" He consulted the GPS.

Ex-green beret Crutchlow squatted, examining the ground. "These tire tracks are fresh. There were definitely four. One of these minis continued that way." The others stood over him, red lights training on the tread impressions leading southwest. "For sure, one of those cars," he said, jabbing a thumb behind.

"Alright," Perkins said, tucking the GPS away. "We'll follow this trail. It's going in the right direction. We'll go until sunrise. If we find nothing by then, we'll make camp."

An hour later, they came upon a hunk of debris resting on the trail. Closer inspection told them it was a piece of aircraft. The Eastern sky was faintly glowing, illuminating the surrounding region. Adjacent the road, the blackened earth smoldered. They made out larger portions of an airplane, like a macabre arrangement of tombstones.

Perkin's sub-gun hung by a tactical strap on his belly. He rested his hands on the weapon and mulled over the situation. He gazed ahead. "I don't know what this means, but I'm going to assume it happened after this mini passed through. Let's move on."

8

"This is becoming the creepiest op ever," Moreland said as he fell in line behind Perkins.

"Yeah, no joke," Perkins said. "It's been a shitshow from the start. Chi-Hye will be lucky if she's alive still."

The trail angled west gradually. Half an hour later, they stood at the edge of a hard-packed dirt road running north and south. Headlights sparkled on the horizon. The team vanished into the scrub and rocks. A semi-truck rumbled passed without incident.

On his belly, Perkins rose to his knees and settled back on his ankles, hands on hips. *The sun will be up soon. No time to press on.* "We'll stop here, rest, and watch this road for a while." He gestured to a knoll fifty meters from the road. "Over there. Let's setup on the other side."

"What about our mystery vehicle trail?" Crutchlow asked. "It crossed over the road."

"I dunno. There's a mothballed base out here in this area. It was super-secret for a long time. This road." Perkins sawed at his chin. "These trucks. Out here in the middle of nowhere. Seems fishy to me." He held a hand out to Roberts, who deftly hauled Perkins up.

"So, we're not following the trail anymore?" Crutchlow asked, pulling his watch cap off and scratching his scalp.

"I think this car and road go to the same place. We'll see how much traffic goes by. Might be some military stuff that'll give us a hint."

The party moved to the knoll and laid behind it. Tired from hours of hiking and lack of sleep, they rolled up inside their ponchos.

"Wish we had somewhere to hang our hammocks. This ground is gonna be *hace frío*," Fernandez said as he stripped off his pack.

Perkins took the first watch since he'd had a decent sleep right before leaving. The others snoozed, but nobody got any good sleep. *Just another night on the job. Wonder what everybody is doing back home?*

Images of the shredded kids in the cars made him shiver. Guilt washed over him for leaving Chi-Hye in a fit of anger. He wasn't a coward or buddy-fucker. *So, why'd I bail?* His ill-fated decision would haunt him forever if she got killed. *It's that stupid Mossad agent, Gruben. If he'd just listened to reason.* Perkins frowned. *That doesn't change the fact I left her in danger.* He breathed a heavy sigh. *Nothing we can do now but track 'em down. We'll either rescue her or find out what happened.*

II

The CIA paramilitary operators staked out the back country road for two hours. In that time, three semi-trucks rumbled north and seven headed south. The temporary road didn't strike one as a shipping route. Unpaved and remote, trucks didn't do well on rough roads. Wherever the vehicles were going, it wasn't a normal operation, and it needed a lot of outside support. One of the departing trucks hauled an open container overflowing with garbage. A tattered net barely held the trash from flying out. Perkins crumpled a corn chip bag he'd picked up and tossed it. He whistled for a huddle.

On their bellies, facing each other in a circle, the team discussed their observations.

"I wanna hi-jack one of those trucks and go south," Perkins said, eyes flicking from face to face. "See where it's going, at least."

Moreland rubbed at his nose. "Maybe we could stowaway."

"Problem there," Crutchlow said, "how do we get a truck to slow down long enough to climb aboard?"

Moreland shook his head, curled one corner of his mouth and fiddled with a pebble. "I don't know? Pull my pant leg up and hope they like my hairy legs?"

Crutchlow pursed his lips. "Nah. They'd mistake you for a corpse as pale as you are. There's enough rock around. We can set up a barricade across the road."

Native to Alaska, Moreland wasn't offended by Crutchlow's quip. He'd joined the navy out of high school, went to BUDS (Basic Underwater Demolition School) and became a SEAL (Sea, Air, and Land). In his spare time, he completed an online degree in law enforcement. Tired of being wet and freezing his ass off, he didn't re-enlist. Moreland figured he'd end up a cop or border patrol. Instead, he signed up with the CIA. SEALs didn't see half the action he did with the CIA. They kept one busy.

Perkins, nodding, said, "I agree. Best we can do is stop one and interrogate the driver." Pointing a finger at Fernandez and Roberts, he said, "What do you two think?"

"Sounds good to me," Fernandez said.

Tate Roberts responded likewise. Roberts always dreamed of being in Delta Force. The United States Army made sure he didn't get too dreamy. First, he endured boot camp in July. Afterward, he found out you couldn't just join Delta Force. Pissed he had to slog through a few years in the regular army, Roberts put his all into an airborne application. A year later, he was jumping from an airplane in his first of two test jumps. Passing with flying colors, he immediately applied to Delta Force. Another brutal test regime for Delta gave him a case of heat exhaustion. It was looking more and more like he'd just be regular army. Then a man in a suit paid him a visit and offered a job with the CIA.

"Alright," Perkins said, "Let's get close by the road, gather our rocks and set up a roadblock." He held a fist out. The others bumped it and moved out to their tasks.

Two decades after setting up shop in Nuremberg, Germany, Lin Yuhan and his wife, Ren, weren't happy with their next assignment from the Chinese Ministry of State Security. As a 'reward' for their heroic service as illegals in Germany, the two MSS agents got assigned driving a supply route for a secret operation in Mongolia. When they received the new orders, Ren had clutched Lin's arm as his mouth opened to protest. Her steadying hand held his anger in check; she knew as well as her husband that making them truck drivers was an insult. It was orders and orders were orders. He begrudgingly complied, even though he was sure their future would be a gloomy one.

Their truck was new, well-appointed for the trip, including a two-person sleeping compartment. Mongolia presented a beautiful and remote landscape, far from people and civilization. By the first day's end, both their attitudes had changed for the better. They were enjoying themselves like a retired couple cruising on a land-yacht.

Ren, reading aloud in Mandarin from a tablet PC screen resting in her lap, said, "Where was Napoleon Bonaparte exiled to the second time?" She looked up from the screen at Lin, who stared out the windshield contemplatively, hands resting together on the steering wheel's lower rim.

Lin stroked at his chin. "The first time was Elba. The second time was... Helen or Helena? Something like that."

Ren smiled and bowed her head. "Very good, husband. I was thinking of Corsica."

Lin settled back in his seat, a smug smile creasing his face. They played a trivia game to pass the time on their long hauls. Both Lin and Ren knew how to operate a tractor trailer. Driving all day took some getting used to. Trekking thousands of kilometers across Mongolian steppe land was another thing. A driving duo made the haul less arduous. Their only genuine concern was whether this would hamper their advancement prospects in the Ministry of State Security. *Is being tasked to truck driving duties a demotion?* Lin asked himself that question every day.

"At least this road is straight and easy," Lin said, gesturing an up-turned palm toward the open road. "But would it have killed them to pave the fucking thing?"

Ren shook her head. "Paving it would have made it stand out—what's that?" She stabbed a finger dead ahead.

Lin saw the dark line a kilometer out, stretching across the road. He let off the gas and down shifted. The exhaust brake growled. A minute later, they rolled to a stop. Their dust plume caught up and swirled around the halted semi. A line of rocks, each about the size of a human head, spanned the road ten meters in front.

Lin, leaning forward, said, "What the hell is this shit?"

Ren unbuckled her seat belt and scooted forward, resting a hand on the dashboard, scanning outside. "Someone's set up a roadblock. Must be bandits." She twisted behind her seat and brought out an AK-74 rifle with a retractable stock, charged the breech, and left the stock retracted. Both MSS agents peered around the vicinity.

"They're waiting for us to get out." He turned to Ren. "Or maybe they've gone away. I'm going to get out. If nobody comes, I'll move enough rocks so we can get past."

"Well, maybe we should--," Ren said, concern clear in her eyes.

"No. If we hesitate, they'll have us. I will hurry."

Ren chewed on her cheek and nodded.

Lin unbuckled his seat belt, grasped the door handle and, turning back to Ren, he nodded. She bobbed her head. He inhaled a deep breath, yanked the handle, and leaned on the door. Ren tensed, panning the gun barrel all around. She rolled down her window for a better view rearward. Lin slid out of the truck, slammed the door shut and crouched by the fuel tank. Casting a furtive glance behind, he loped to the rock line and began rolling a stone to the road's edge. Two minutes later, he had a gap wide enough for their truck.

Hands on hips, Lin surveyed the opening. With a nod, he trotted back to the truck. As he reached for the door handle, a black-clad figure emerged from behind the truck's cab, sub-gun trained on Lin, whose mouth gaped.

"Don't move, motherfucker," Crutchlow said.

Lin froze. *They're Americans?*

"Keep your hands where I can see them," Crutchlow said, as he hopped down and closed the distance. A second hijacker followed close behind the first. "You speak English?"

Lin narrowed his eyes. *They look like Baader's people. If I speak English, maybe I can talk our way out of this.* "Yes," he said, glancing at the truck's door. "My wife inside. She armed."

American eyes and guns trained up toward the driver's door.

Crutchlow stepped close to the fuel tank, eyes frequently flicking up at the window, and keyed his mic. "There's at least one armed woman inside."

"Roger that. We've got this side covered."

Gesturing at Lin with his gun's barrel, Crutchlow indicated the door. "Tell her to come out peacefully and no one gets hurt."

Lin swallowed, hoping Ren wouldn't open fire on them instantly. The older Asian man nodded, locked eyes with Crutchlow and, slow as a chameleon, reached for the door handle. "Wife," he called. "Don't shoot. It's okay. I'm opening door now. Hold fire, okay?"

Lin grasped the door handle, listening for a response. He pulled the handle, unlatching the door. Slowly, he swung it open. Inside, Ren sat wide-eyed, hands raised, with the gun out of sight. They made eye contact.

Moreland stepped behind Lin, resting a restraining hand on his shoulder. "Stay here, buddy. But tell her to come out. Slowly."

Lin nodded rapidly, holding his hands up. "They want you out." She nodded, lowering a hand and opening her door. A minute later, both MSS Officers stood, backs to the front bumper, facing five American agents dressed in all black like the First People of Evolution anarchists. Lin was keenly aware of the FPE, having dealt with their leader, Herman Baader, in an arms deal. But something was off. *I thought Baader only recruited Germans?*

Arms folded, sub-gun dangling at his side, Perkins stepped to the pair. He stroked his chin for a moment, narrowing his eyes. "Where are you going? What's in your truck?"

Ren and Lin exchanged a glance, but remained silent. Perkins unfolded his arms and casually backhanded Lin with a resounding *SLAP*. His head lolled until he faced Perkins, blood seeping from the corner of his mouth, fury written across his face. He dabbed at it with a hand. "We're just truck drivers. They tell us nothing except 'get this here and take it there.'" Lin's eyes flicked to Perkins, malice showing in his knitted brows.

Perkins refolded his arms. "I'm going to need more than that." He moved in front of Ren. Lin tensed. Eyeing the Chinese woman, Perkins asked, "Where are you going? What's in your truck?"

The tense Chinese intelligence officer remained stoic. She glared at Perkins. "All they give us is address."

Perkins was incredulous. "An address? Out here? Who's they?"

Again, Lin and Ren kept quiet, so Perkins slapped her across the face. Lin hugged his wife to himself. "Stop! She knows nothing. Don't hurt her."

Perkins shot a glance and nod at Roberts and Moreland. They stepped to Lin, taking him by the arms. "Let's try this again. I'm going to beat the both of you to death if someone doesn't start talking. We can do this all day. And toss your bodies out for the vultures." He took a lock of Ren's hair in one hand, rubbing it between two fingers and leering. Then the CIA man abruptly grabbed her hair at the side of her head.

The woman cried out. Lin swore and struggled in futile fashion with Moreland and Roberts. Glancing back at Lin, Perkins raised a fist aimed at Ren.

"Okay! Okay!" Lin cried. "I'll talk. We're going mountain bunker. We're just hauling supplies. We're just truck drivers. Please, don't hurt my wife. We only just started."

Perkins, fist still held aloft, flexed his knuckles. "What else?"

Lin, sputtering for words, said, "Wh—that's it. It's the truth. Please don't hurt us."

Fernandez climbed inside the truck and began rifling through it. He leaned his head out. "There's nothing interesting in here. Well, except for a Kalashnikov behind the passenger seat. A walkie-talkie and some food." He stood between the door and the cab above them.

Perkins mulled over their captives, looking Ren up and down. "Yeah, that should work." He looked at Fernandez. "Hey, come down here and try this chick's coat on. I got an idea."

Fernandez shrugged, hopping down.

Perkins waggled fingers at Ren, pantomiming doffing her coat. "We'll be needing your coat."

"Deel," Lin corrected.

Perkins cocked an eyebrow. "Deel. Whatever. Hand it over."

Their Chinese prisoner reluctantly removed her garment, a traditional Mongolian 'deel' that crossed over the front of the body and tied at the waist, this one lined with wool. Underneath, she wore a plain white button-down shirt. She held the deel out.

Fernandez came by and took it, flinging it over his back and jamming a hand into one arm. Once he had both arms in, he secured it across the front and turned a circle while tugging on the arm cuffs. "It's warm, but doesn't fit me for shit."

"Yeah," Perkins said, putting hands on hips. "But it'll do. You'll ride shotgun up front with old-boy here. Keep him straight and make sure he doesn't rat us out."

Fernandez peered at the truck. "What? Why?"

"Because you're the only one with a tan that looks remotely Asian."

Fernandez shook his head. "Man, that's racist."

"I'll give you racist: us white guys will ride in back while you brownies chauffeur us around." He spread a toothy grin. "Mrs.—hey, what's your names?"

Lin and Ren exchanged a glance. Lin finally locked eyes with Perkins. "My name is Jackie. Hers is Lucy."

Perkins snorted. "Yeah, right? Jackie Chan and Lucy Liu? Brilliant." He shrugged. "Those'll have to do. As I was saying, Lucy will ride in back with us." He jabbed a thumb at the trailer. Lin glared at Perkins. "She'll be our insurance. Because we're going where this truck goes—into the mountain. Something is going on at that old base. We need to find out what." He slapped a hand on Jackie's shoulder. "Come on, Jackie, get behind the wheel. Lucy, you're with us."

"We should check-in," Crutchlow said.

While Roberts, Moreland, and Crutchlow inspected the trailer, Perkins keyed his mic. "Crow's Nest, this is Raven One."

A pause. Static. "Go ahead, Raven One."

"Crow's nest, we've acquired transportation. Following the trail south."

"Roger that, Raven One."

The Americans found a trailer full of dry goods like toilet paper and canned goods. Fernandez latched the doors shut once everyone was aboard, and trotted back to the cab, where he scaled inside with Jackie.

III

Discomfort registered in Karl Gruben's brain. His wrists ached. The orange coveralls issued to him wreaked of every body odor. But hunger consumed most of his thoughts. They starved him the first couple of days, providing a cup of water in the morning, at lunch and the evening. Meal times came once a day after the initial starvation. A paper plate of cold rice got shoved through a rectangular opening centered in the cell's door. Karl woofed down the food, uncaring of its origin and condition. It was food and his body demanded anything edible nowadays. Afterward, it occurred to him they might poison or drug the rice. *What difference would refusing food make? Dead by poisoning would be at least faster than by starvation. I'm not ready to die. Best to keep my strength up.*

Gruben's thoughts drifted in and out of consciousness. He cracked his eyes opened, then quickly shut them. Debilitating grogginess threatened to overwhelm him. Seated alone in a metal chair, Karl rolled his shoulders and head, eyes fluttering. Lack of visual cues disoriented him. A light behind, low, on the floor. The room was dark, otherwise lit only by the lamp. He twisted around and glimpsed a flashlight lying on the gray concrete floor.

Powerful emotions unfolded: fear, anger, hopelessness. His handcuffs clinked against the chair's backside, the steel restraints snug on his skin, unyielding. Scuffling behind brought him fully aware.

"Good, you're awake," A man said. "Tell me more about your mission assignments." The flashlight suddenly rolled. Chair leg shadows danced on the concrete wall.

Karl squinted. *Can't tell how many there are. One? Two?*

"Are they always in dog shit?"

Dread poured over Karl like cold mud. *They know about the SD card containers? How long has it been? How many times have I gotten drugged, dragged from my cell and brought here? What have I told them?*

Shoes scuffled behind. "Your friends told me all about what you do. They're returning to America and Israel soon." The man snorted. "Diplomacy at work. But you—you're not going anywhere." He clucked his tongue. "You fucked everything up, Gruben. I mean, really fucked them up." A hand rested on either of Karl's shoulders. Abruptly, the voice was close to Karl's ear. "Just between you and me, though, it's okay. I didn't like the idea of Bubonic plague running rampant in the wild." The breath is warm, smelling of cigarettes.

Karl shifted slightly, cutting his eyes at the fingers, keeping his face forward. *Did he say plague? The plane. Baader. They were escorting a virus somewhere…*

One hand lifted and twirled in a circle. "Too likely it would blow back our way." The hands disappeared. Scuffling and then the light moved crazily. Another snort. "You even burned it to a crisp. If only you could see the blackened crash site." He clucked his tongue again. "China will win a war of attrition. Because when you've got a billion citizens, you've got some fat to burn. Your friends agreed and have already gone home to their families."

Piqued, Karl lifted his head. "They're free?" Illogical as his mind said it was, his gut sank with betrayal. *How could they leave me behind? Where's the Institute and CIA?* "Why can't I go home?"

The flashlight rolled. Shadows cycled in the other direction. "Oh, yes, they're free because they cooperated with us. You, though, are stubborn or stupid." The man chuckled. "Which is it? A pigheaded fool or intellectually challenged? I doubt you're stupid. Mossad isn't in the habit of employing dumb asses." He kicked the flashlight. Chair leg shadows flicked across the wall like a watch in fast forward. "They can't believe you've chosen to be so uncooperative. They're worried, Karl. Worried their comrade has lost his mind—lost his nerve. If you don't start talking, they're not going home. Do you want them to suffer more?"

Karl shook his head and knit his eyebrows together. "What—what am I supposed to say? I don't remember what was asked. I thought they already went home?"

He heard whistling through the air like a golf club swinging. *WHACK!* In a flare of star bursts, pain suddenly erupted at the side of his head as it whipped to one side. "Ow!" The blunted haymaker left him disoriented. Scalp stinging, he couldn't help but peer behind, glimpsing a dark-colored baton grasped in a fist. It rose to his face and jabbed at his cheek. He quickly faced forward.

"I'm losing my patience. We could avoid all of this. If you'd just be part of the solution. Right now, you're a problem."

Whoever this is, has decent English. Not a regular soldier.

His tormentor heaved a sigh. "The world, as you knew it, is gone. Though you stopped one prong of the attack, the other arrived at its destination and got released. The economic disaster will level the playing field. All the world will change. For the better, of course."

Karl stiffened.

"Don't worry. We're safe in this isolated facility and we're all immunized." He chuckled. "A virus is spreading across the world as we speak. What do you think about that?" A light whack on Karl's shoulder made him flinch disproportionately.

"The Great Reset has begun."

Virus? Mom? Dad? Gabby? Karl looked over his shoulder. "What are you talking about?"

The flashlight got rolled again.

"A great reset of the world. All its economic and political backbones broken. Futile ideas like capitalism, freedom, and liberty will soon fade away. Those idiotic and archaic western notions of representative government are a house of cards. Rife with corruption and greed. And Israel," he chuckled, "they're surrounded. America won't help either. Not at first. The Zionists will need to pull out the stops. Just like they won't help Taiwan when the time comes. Imagine that, computer microchips are as valuable as oil now. And we've got the number one manufacturer of semiconductors just off our coast. Your friends grasped that concept quickly. Eagerly even. Open up, Gruben.

24

Tell me about your knowledge of this facility. How did you find it? Make it easy on yourself. There's no reason to resist, because you're already lost."

Arnold? Kevin? Tonya? Why would you give into this? How could you give into it? Well, dumb ass, they got shot, maimed, captured, and here I am, doubting their loyalty and fortitude. I'm no better.

From not far away, a man screamed.

Karl stiffened. *That sounded like Arnold! They're lying. They haven't capitulated. They are not free. But I'll break soon. None of us can hold out indefinitely. Hunger is maddening. The drugs. The interrogation. There's got to be a way.* He hung his head, chin resting on his chest. *I just need one chance.* Karl followed the pacing shadows behind him. With his hands bound, it was unlikely he could overpower this guy. Once he did, where would he go next? He couldn't trust anything his tormentor said, but by implication, the man told Karl he was still in the Mongolian mountain base.

Scuffling. The man always stayed out of reach.

Not close enough to try. Must be ready for my chance.

IV

Twenty minutes after hijacking Jackie and Lucy's tractor trailer, a low mountain loomed on the horizon. Fernandez, riding shotgun wearing Lucy's dingy blue deel, kept a suppressed 9mm pistol concealed under the coat, aimed at the driver. The sun was shining over a cloudless sky. A blue dome spanned above. Brown, rocky, unforgiving terrain surrounded them.

Seldom at a loss for words, Jackie's flare for profanity did not fail him, frequently pelting Fernandez with a string of explicates. Annoyed but focused, Fernandez ignored the man's protestations. Between Mandarin and English curses, he gathered they were nearing their destination.

Fernandez keyed a walkie under his coat. "We're approaching something. What do you wanna do?" He wore a single, wired earbud in his right ear. It burbled with encryption noise.

Perkin's tinny voice said, "Check. Bad guys?"

A quick glance around, then Fernandez said, "Negative." He eyed Jackie, who glared back.

Jackie flicked a finger ahead. In English, he said, "Camouflage entrance."

Fernandez sat straight, leaning forward, one hand going on the dash. "Entrance? Entrance to what?"

Jackie stared ahead, hands at 10 o'clock and 2 o'clock

on the over-sized steering wheel. He pulled in a deep breath, turning to Fernandez, who stared back askance. Reluctance written on his face, Jackie said, "Entrance to underground facility. Unit 57." He broke the gaze. *They'll be caught in minutes once inside.*

Fernandez scowled. "Unit 57? What's that? Can we get inside?" He tightened his grip on the pistol.

Jackie, with a blank look on his face, said, "It is secret base. One of many. This one old, though."

"Are there troops? Stop the truck." He keyed his mic. "Hey, this guy says we're going to some underground base. I told him—."

Jackie interrupted his report, patting the air with one hand. "It's okay. We don't need stop. If we stop, might draw attention. They let us inside," he said with a dismissive hand wave. "What are you doing here, anyway?"

"Told him what?" Perkins said in Fernandez's ear. He cocked his head toward the mic. "We're looking for someone," Fernandez answered Jackie's question, then keyed his radio. "Hey, standby. Looks like we'll be getting inside this place. Hang tight."

"Roger that."

"Who are you looking for?" Jackie asked with a furtive glance at Fernandez.

"A woman. An American. Possibly some others. Know anything about them?"

Jackie shook his head. "No." He turned to the Hispanic agent. "They no hurt my wife, will they? I cooperate. Help you. As long as you don't harm me or her."

They locked eyes. Finally shaking his head, Fernandez said, "No, man, we won't hurt her. But if you try something…" He shook his head and broke the stare.

Jackie nodded.

After a minute of silence, the road cleared a rock formation, heading toward a steep portion on the mountain's side. It rose a hundred meters high and was at least three hundred wide. Where the road intersected the cliff face, a seam opened, growing larger as a camouflaged garage door moved aside, the interior contrasting darkly with the brightly lit landscape. Another truck exited from the shadowed opening. It rumbled past them as they approached. An armed sentry, holding out an arm, waited for Jackie to stop.

"Just let me do talking," Jackie said, holding a finger up. "Their security bad. I tell them too. But they won't listen."

Fernandez nodded and tried acting casual. He knew about three words in Mandarin—all of them profanity. If Jackie were slick and he betrayed them, Fernandez wouldn't know it. Instead, he would just have to watch Jackie's and the guard's body language.

They came to a halt with a hiss of pneumatic brake pressure release and dust. Jackie rolled his window down, laying an arm casually on the sill. The guard's head popped up at the open window. They greeted each other matter-of-factually; the man giving Fernandez a cursory glance. Jackie handed over his bill of lading and documentation. After a minute, the guard, satisfied all was in order, hopped down.

Fernandez couldn't take his eyes off the dark interior of this cavernous operation. *What the hell goes on here?* To their left, he saw a much larger set of sliding hangar doors. They were closed at the moment. Inside, personnel moved hither and thither, most wearing blue coveralls and yellow helmets. The stench of trapped diesel exhaust permeated the air. He sawed at his chin and relaxed his white-knuckle grip on the pistol. *Stay calm. The others are in back. I'm not alone and we're not walking into a trap. I hope.*

Jackie revved the engine and feathered the clutch. They eased forward out of the bright sunlight, into the massive cavern, easily thirty meters high, its ceiling dotted with powerful white LED lights. The road stretched back into the complex. Fernandez spotted a set of rolling stairs and realized the road was, in reality, a runway. *Connects this place to the crash site.* He keyed his mic. "We're past security and going inside a—a cavern. A complex in the mountainside."

"Roger that."

Half a dozen trucks backed up to a loading dock on their right. A blue cover-all clad man directed Jackie to an empty spot at the loading dock between two other trailers. Jackie, new to tractor-trailer driving, sucked at backing up. He positioned the truck and stopped to drop it into reverse. Hand on the gearshift, eyes on the mirrors, he said, "I just started driving trucks, so shut the fuck up about my reverse."

"Trucks are easy to back up, man," Fernandez said, peering at the mirror on his side. "Just take it slow. I'll help. Back her up."

Jackie ground his teeth. Helping the enemy galled him. The enemy being helpful pissed him off even more. He growled and slapped the transmission into reverse, focusing on his mirrors. The truck eased backward.

"That's it, keep it coming," Fernandez said, left hand waving backward. A few seconds later he said, "Nope. You're too far left. Come right. Nope. Aw, man, you fucked it." He turned from the mirror to Jackie. "You're out of whack. Pull forward and try again."

Jackie's eyebrows were almost touching, his brow so furrowed. They repeated this process four times before finally getting the trailer slipped in between the other ones.

Perkins and the others investigated the trailers contents during the ride. Many large wooden crates and pallets piled with supplies and wrapped in plastic filled it from front to back. Feeling trapped in the confined space, they pried open a few crates in search of hiding places. They selected three, contorting themselves around the items inside. The truck had lurched forward and back half a dozen times. Only Perkins remained outside of a box when the trailer bumped hard into a loading dock. He shook his head. *About damned time.*

Perkins peered through a small hole near the back door. Upon seeing a yellow forklift ready on the loading dock, he hurried to a crate. Pausing, he keyed his mic. "Crow's Nest, Raven One."

Static.

"Crow's Nest, Raven One."

Static.

"Damn, no signal getting out of this place."

Jackie opened his door. Before exiting, he looked over at Fernandez. "I must speak with the dock manager." He waggled his paperwork at Fernandez. "Their security suck, but they keep paperwork. Bastards! Hey, you don't think your friends shoot?"

Fernandez lifted his chin, then shrugged and reached for his door.

"No!" Jackie said, eyes wide. "No shootout! You stay here. Tell them hide!"

Door ajar, Fernandez nodded and settled back into his seat. "Yeah, okay. Lemme check." He keyed his mic. "Hey, you guys need to hide. They're gonna unload the truck."

"Check." Perkins said, "We're already in some crates."

"Roger that." Fernandez nodded at Jackie. "They're outta sight."

Perkins said, "There's a crew ready to unload. Everybody stay quiet." Muffles affirmations replied. He spun around, casting a flashlight beam along the side of the cargo-filled trailer. With alacrity, the paramilitary operative and Lucy, whose hands were still bound, squeezed into a crate. They contorted themselves around an electric pump strapped to the crate's bottom. He carefully laid the lid into place. As the last bit of dim light extinguished in their crate, he made eye contact with Lucy, holding a finger to his lips. She gave a quick nod.

Roberts and Moreland tucked in together while Crutchlow rode solo in a third container. Seconds later came the rolling door's rattle. Tense and ready, Perkins wiped away a trickle of sweat coursing down his temple.

Fernandez observed Jackie and the dock crew by using the truck's mirrors. He heard the roll-up door open, saw the forklift pull forward. It picked up the first load, backed up, about faced, and carried it through a large opening ten meters back from the loading dock's edge. The truck shook and sank some as the forklift returned, driving inside the trailer this time. Twenty minutes later, the cargo was unloaded. Some of the crates got stacked on a train of small trailers. A flat yellow tractor, like those used at airports, pulled them.

Fernandez didn't know which boxes his comrades were inside. He sat back and ran a hand down his face. *What the hell am I gonna do? How am I gonna to find the others?*

Shoe scuffles outside brought him alert. It was Jackie. The diminutive Asian stopped at his door, peering up at him and pressing eyeglasses up the bridge of his nose.

"Hey!" Fernandez hissed. "Where the hell did they take everybody? We gotta go get them."

Jackie placed one foot on the bottom step and raised a placating hand. "Don't lose shit. Right now, we blend in. I saw crates. Pretty sure I know which them." He gave a furtive glance between trucks toward the loading dock. "Come on. Truck stay here. There's waiting area we can use. I need pee." Jackie backed away from the truck's step-side so Fernandez could exit.

The lightly tanned agent jumped down and held out a hand. "After you." He didn't like this guy leading the way. There wasn't much choice. At least they still had his wife as leverage. Perkins and the others could handle themselves.

They clambered onto the loading dock. Fernandez watched the trailer-train disappear around a corner. "Where are they going? We need to follow them." He took a step in that direction, but Jackie's slender hand caught him at the elbow.

"No!" Jackie said, brow furrowed.

Fernandez glanced at Jackie's hand on his arm. His eyes met Jackie's. Fernandez's eyebrow cocked. Jackie let go.

Jackie, wringing his hands, said, "Please. I promise we find them. My wife with them, and I don't want her getting in crossfire." He gestured a hand gun. "I promise. Now, please, come and try acting like you normal."

Fernandez froze, shooting a hand to his ear.

Nestled in their stuffy crates, Perkins watched outside through a crack between boards. "Fernandez," he hissed into his mic.

A few seconds later, Fernandez's static distorted voice said, "You guys okay?"

"Yeah, we're inside the crates. No idea where we're being taken."

Static.

"Fernandez, you getting this?"

Static.

"Shit. Can't get a signal. Too much rock in the way now." He gave up and settled in for their ride.

It looked like they were doing circles in a parking garage. Despite his best efforts, he couldn't keep track of where they went, given his limited view. Before long, the trip ended at a pair of open double doors. A small forklift came out of the doorway and quickly unloaded the cargo, whereupon the empty trailer-train moved away with an electric whine.

Someone neatly laid them in a row.

Perkins keyed his mic. "Okay, looks like we've

reached our destination. Time to--." He glimpsed four Asian men shuffling into the room. "We've got company. Looks like a workshop here. Hang on."

Another man entered the room and said, "These are the boxes. Uncrate the equipment inside. I'll be back in one hour." He narrowed his eyes. "And it better be done by then, or I'll report you." The workers scratched at their heads, grumbled, and inspected the crates. Their boss spun on a heel and left the room.

"Alright," Perkins said, "The main guy left. There's just four dudes. We're gonna have to take 'em out. Everybody ready?"

"Roger that," Moreland said.

Crutchlow said, "Let's light 'em up. I can't breathe in here."

"Roger that," Perkins said. "On three, then. One. Two. Three!"

Before the work crew's eyes, three crate lids flipped open and four men rose out, suppressed pistols drawn. The workers became wide-eyed statues. In stilted Mandarin, Perkins said, "Hands up!" The workers exchanged a glance, lifting their arms in confusion. One of them bolted for the door, but Crutchlow clothes-lined him, slamming the man hard onto his back. He kneeled and clocked him with his gun. The blue coverall-clad man went limp.

While the other workers gawked in horror, the team closed in on them. They began shouting. Arms quickly snaked around necks. In less than thirty seconds, all the workers were dead.

Perkins assessed the situation. "Roberts, watch the door. Moreland, help me get the crates unloaded. Crutch get these guys stripped. We're gonna need their outfits."

Thirty minutes later, Perkins set the last crate lid back into place, leaning on the container and wiping his brow. "You guys need to change clothes." He stared at Lucy. "You too."

Face of stone, Lucy glared at Perkins as she bent and picked up the smallest of the over-sized coveralls. Scrutinizing them with a crinkled nose. "These are disgusting."

"Yeah," Moreland breathed, "I'm not super happy about wearing someone else's clothes either." He looked at Perkins. "Hey, what are you gonna wear?"

"I'm staying in this outfit, hedging our bets as part of security."

"Aw, man. I wanna be in security," Crutchlow whined.

"Not this time, bro." Perkins sauntered over to Crutchlow and straightened the photo ID badge clipped to his coveralls. "These should make suitable cover if no one checks them closely." He surveyed the workshop. "Let's hide our gear in one of these cabinets for now."

Moreland, knocking on a crate, asked, "What are we gonna do with the bodies?"

"We'll figure that out later," Perkins replied, glancing at his watch. "This guy will return soon. If we fool him, then I'd say we're good to go."

"Good to go where?" Crutchlow asked as he pulled his coverall zipper up.

Perkins shrugged. "Stay tuned. We need to find Fernandez and the driver." He keyed his mic, glancing at Lucy, who turned away. "Fernandez. You copy?"

Static.

Roberts, watching the door, stepped away backward. "Someone's coming. Get ready." They concealed their pistols and tried to act like they were just finishing up.

The door opened. It was the supervisor. He strode into the room, drawing a deep breath. Abruptly, he stopped and stared at the work crew, eyes stopping on the black-clad Perkins. Scowling, hands going to hips, in Mandarin he asked, "Who are you?"

Perkins cleared his throat. In hideous Mandarin, he said, "We new men. Better men."

Dubious, the man scratched at his cheek. "New men? Better men? Where did you learn Chinese? Your words sound like two cats fucking."

Comprehending only the supervisor's English swear words, Perkins shrugged and stepped toward the man, arms spread. "Not many Mandarin words."

Moreland surreptitiously moved behind the man.

The supervisor nodded as he took in the status of the crates. "You unloaded these?"

Perkins, understanding the man's gestures more than understanding his words, said, "Yes. We take out." He gestured toward the freshly removed equipment laying neatly in a row on the floor.

A smile split the supervisor's face. He slapped Perkins on the shoulder. "Ha! You did a great job. And fast. The last crew was the laziest and dumbest labor personnel I've ever had to work with." He spun and grabbed the door handle.

Moreland inspected his fingernails.

The supervisor called over his shoulder. "I thought they would take all afternoon." He pulled open the door. "You can take the rest of the day off. You did such a good job."

Perkins made eye contact with the man and nodded profusely. "Thank you, sir. Thank you."

The man gave a curt nod, darting from the room.

Moreland shrugged. "I was about to grab him, but it looked like he was just gonna leave with no hassle, so I didn't risk making him disappear."

"Good thinking," Perkins said, nodding.

V

Tingling in Karl's right arm and abdomen brought him around. He was lying face down on a thin mattress, his arm pinned under himself. He gingerly rolled, extracting the limb. For a long few minutes, the imprisoned Mossad agent lay motionless, save the methodical flexing of his right hand. Gradually, the fog faded, and he fully perceived his prison cell. The one where he lived, not the one where they tormented him. *How long can a person endure drugs? Day in and day out. How many days has it been?*

Karl rolled onto his back, studying the drab gray ceiling. The quiet solitude embraced him, comforted him. There is peace when there is silence. His captors were gone for the day. *Or night. I wish I could tell.* In the early days, he would awaken and begin inspecting every crevice of his cell. It was easy to find where he'd left off. As the days and nights, strung together with long interrogations, melded into one; he couldn't tell anymore. So he began searching anew.

The heavy steel door squelched most sounds from outside. He detected guards when they came for him or brought food. Footsteps and the beeping of the keypad. No other prisoner sounds except what he heard earlier. His cell probing never located a microphone or camera hole. Which made him assume they didn't spy on him.

Or that was what they wanted him thinking. That made him more paranoid, imagining devices were there. Hidden so well, he just couldn't find them.

The inability to discern where and when was fraying the edges of his sanity. He knew time was crawling, but without a reference it seemed to have stopped all together.

With a heave, Karl raised himself upright. The pressure on his bladder triggered a critical mass warning. He rose from the bed and shuffled to the stainless steel toilet. Spattering urine loud in the absence of other sounds. Relieved, and still drowsy, he took in some deep breaths and wind milled his arms a few times. He rested his hands on his hips, eyeing the cold concrete floor. They hadn't broken his body, not yet anyway, which permitted him the ability to exercise. Hungry, thirsty, and weary, he lowered to all fours, extended his legs and began a regimen of push-ups.

After a few sets, Karl switched to sit-ups. The exercises were lethargic motions. A man willing himself to keep going. To keep his strength up. To kill time. Minutes later, lying on his back on the floor, abdominal exercises finished, he climbed to his feet and stepped to the door. It had a ten centimeter by fifty centimeter hatch about waist level. His food came through the hatch and he also put his arms through for cuffing and needle jab. *Why the sedation every time? They must have hundreds, if not thousands, of personnel. A few escorts would be plenty, given my restraints. Are they worried I might take them all on? The times I resisted, even a little, they beat the crap out of me. There were too many goons.*

He rubbed at the back of his sore head, winced, raising his arms to the door's top frame. It jutted out two centimeters from the wall. *Not the best grip. Enough for a few pull-ups.*

The truncheons they used on him didn't break bones, but they stung and hurt like hell. Karl stopped after three pull-ups, about faced, then leaned back against the door. After catching his breath, he leaned off the door and faced it. He stooped and fiddled with the hatch. The hinges were on the outside. It was just a faint rectangular outline on the door. Eyeing the handle, he gripped it and gave it a tug. It didn't even jiggle in the door frame. *But, hey, you never know. Somebody might forget to lock it one day.*

He stood and leaned back again on the door, arms folded. After a moment, he closed his eyes, laying his head back on the cold metal door. It felt good on his sore skin.

Karl visualized his surroundings, the corridor without and the route they took him. The process was foggy. Sedation kicked in when they ushered him out of the cell and down a shadowy hallway. Light from too few overhead lights made the experience even more disorienting. It reminded Karl of strobe lit tunnels in haunted houses. All glimpses and snapshots. Here, then gone, always just out of grasp.

There are stairs. Yes, at the corridor's end. There are other cells along the way. He ran a hand through his hair and felt stubble. Shocked, both hands flew to his head, rubbing it all over. "They shaved my damn head! Fucking bastards!" He squeezed his eyes shut and refocused on his mental excursion, idly fingering the stubble. *After the stairs—they open up one, maybe two, levels down. Several doors on that level. Fucking assholes! They shaved my damned head.* He palmed his face. *I'm never getting out of here. I'll die here alone.*

A few steps is all it took getting to his meager bed, which comprised a stainless steel shelf with a thin mattress, no pillow. Karl flopped onto his back, laying an arm across his forehead. *What happened to the others? I know Fang is lying. I heard Arnold. I'm sure of it.* In the stillness, Karl's self-pity waxed to guilt. *We ran headlong into this—at my command.* He brought his arm down across his eyes. *Am I such a narcissist? Soldiers have fallen in the slaughter for time immemorial. I'm just another leader who is prone to getting his cohorts killed, maimed, and tortured.* His impotence infuriated him. Not being able to 'fix' the situation gnawed at his soul.

The metal bed creaked as he rose from it with a grunt. He began pacing. Five steps up, five steps back. *What follows the stairs?* This phase was much foggier. The sedative would be peaking. *It's short-lived. Just enough to move me.* A vision of emerging from the stairwell coalesced in his mind's eye. It opened into a room or foyer with two doors. They took him to both randomly. *Each cell is identical to the other: a concrete box. Drain at the center. Dark. A chair and a light.*

No other person ever peeked in on the sessions with Karl—no matter how they made him scream in pain and madness. *That room with one person is my best hope. Overpower the one guy and escape. Maybe I can find my team. Maybe I can let them out? The problem is the sedative.* He found himself at the door, leaned back and slid down until he sat, hugging his knees, rubbing at sore wrists. Karl knew his shelf life wasn't unlimited.

Before long, he'd be useless to them. And they don't keep useless things around for long.

VI

The room they were in had a butcher block topped work bench running along each wall. White Formica veneered cabinets above and below. A disemboweled electric motor lay on one bench. Another had a vise attached at one end. Tools hung on a magnetic strip underneath the upper cabinets. Four square wood-topped workbenches took up most of the floor space. The room stank of grease and ozone.

"Roberts, watch the door," Perkins said, gesturing for the others to gather around one of the two-meter square workbenches at the shop's rear. Roberts trotted to the door, cracking it open and peering out.

Perkins, facing the entry point, leaned forward, hands on the table. The others gathered around, tension written on their faces.

"Alright, we're inside this place. Now what?" He swept a hand. "I doubt we can stay here for long. And we gotta find Fernandez. Thoughts?"

Crutchlow, tugging on the identification badge clipped to his cover-all collar, said, "The way I see it, we got these. If we're careful, I bet we can move around pretty easily." Eyebrows up, he surveyed the faces.

Moreland, scratching at his chin, said, "And if it doesn't work?"

Crutchlow raspberried. "Hell, we can bullshit our way out."

"Oh, right, just bullshit our way out of a secret Chinese military base. Knowing precious little Mandarin other than 'new men' and 'fucking.' Hard telling what those two phrases will get us into."

"Doesn't look very Chi-comm to me," Crutchlow said, ignoring Moreland's concerns. "Lots of non-Chinese running around."

Perkins said, "Yeah, this place is odd, but he's got a point. We can't stay here and we've gotta do something about those bodies." He glanced at the closed crates, now with four corpses inside. "If we don't do some recon, we'll never know what's going on. Or how to get out of here, or how to fulfill our mission."

The others nodded, falling silent.

Perkins tapped a fingertip on the table. "I think we should go out exploring separately. In different directions. Kinda minimizes our profile. What do you think?"

Moreland turned toward Crutchlow. "We could cover more territory that way."

It wasn't optimal, but nothing was ever optimal. Especially in the field.

"Yeah," Crutchlow said with a shrug. "What are we looking for besides Chi-Hye? What do we do in an emergency?"

They took five minutes piecing together a game plan. Roberts, out of earshot, got clued in by Perkins.

"Man," Roberts said, eyebrows knitting as he groused. "You guys always leave me out of the big votes. Ever notice that?"

Perkins spread his hands. "No. I've never noticed that. You're keeping watch because you were closest to the door. Don't stand so close to the door next time."

"Well, I...," Roberts rubbed his bottom lip with a finger, eyes on the ground. "I didn't really think about it--."

"Never mind," Perkins said, shaking his head. "Everybody meet back here in an hour. Stay out of trouble and take notes. And don't be late." He turned to Ren. "Come on, you're with me."

The team synchronized watches and ventured out, one minute apart.

Perkins and Lucy, last to leave the workshop, strolled along the labyrinth of corridors wordlessly. Lucy was inwardly curious about the complex. Her captivity was proving quite interesting. He kept her close, and on one occasion, reminded her he's armed. Of the people they saw, though, half weren't Chinese. If diversity was what the facility sought, they found it. All races, both male and female, populated the complex. At one point, they watched several weary personnel shuffle through a door. A sign written in English, German, Spanish and Chinese, above the entry said, "Barracks Unit 5."

Perkins, hand on Ren's back, nudged her toward Unit 5. "Come on. Let's check out the barracks." Perkins had to give Lucy credit. She hadn't spoken a word all this time. Unaware she worked for the Chinese Ministry of State Security, he just thought they were entrepreneurs making a buck on a government contract. Her reticence made her unpredictable, though. *I don't trust her any further than I can throw her.*

Inside the barracks, they followed a corridor, dimly lit with red lights for a hundred meters. Doors on either side spaced ten meters apart. The odor of dirty laundry, body odor, and farts filled their nostrils. Perkins sidled up to a door and tried its knob. He smiled at Lucy as the knob turned until he could crack the door. Sounds of tires screeching and music poured out. Peeking through the gap, he saw two guys, backs to him in chairs, watching a movie. They never noticed him, so he gently closed the door. He shewed Lucy further down the hallway, trying knobs now and again. The last few rooms had a set of keys zip-tied to their knobs.

Perkins paused at one, examining the keys before pulling out a pocketknife and cutting them free. He tried a key, furtively glancing up the reddened corridor. The door unlocked, and he pushed it open. Lucy peeked inside the dark room, reaching around the door frame and flicking a light on. Bright white light blazed. Perkins hustled her inside and closed the door.

On either side of the room, a bunk bed sat. Four tall lockers covered the rear wall, and four desks were situated, two on each side, close to the door. All inside a four-meter by four-meter steel reinforced concrete box.

Perkins, hands on hips, circled as he surveyed the unoccupied quad. "Yeah, this'll do nicely." He stepped to the door and pulled it open. Over his shoulder, he said, "Stay put. I'll be right back." Perkins slipped out without waiting for a reply. Or to see if she understood him. He figured she got the point. Thirty seconds later, he returned after inspecting the nearby stairwell leading up and down at the corridor's end.

He dropped the keys in his pants pocket and gestured at Lucy. "Come on. Let's follow these stairs."

The stoic Lucy followed obediently.

No alarms sounded that Fernandez and Jackie knew about. They loitered a few minutes in the driver's lounge before Fernandez grew antsy.

Seated in folding chairs at the room's rear next to Jackie, Fernandez sniffed. He leaned into Jackie. "Hey, you smell food? I smell some grub."

Jackie stared at Fernandez for a moment, then nodded curtly.

Several other drivers must have caught whiff, too. They rose and left.

Fernandez turned to Jackie. "You know where the cafeteria is?"

Jackie hesitated, but he was hungry too. "Yes. It is close."

Jackie rose, Fernandez followed. The pair tailed the recently departed group. Along the way, Fernandez noted placards on walls directing people to various locations—including the cafeteria. The placards showed photographs and, if any words, they were in several languages. It was up ahead on the right.

Entering the dining facility through a set of swinging double doors, Fernandez was relieved it wasn't crowded and disappointed he didn't find his team. He had a futile hope they would be there already. Pairs of individuals sat at long bench tables. The CIA man cocked an eyebrow upon seeing two heavily tattooed men chatting and eating. These two seemed out of place in this facility. The Kanji tats spoke of Yakuza.

He followed Jackie's lead, picking up a food tray from a pile at the food line's end. Eyeing the food laid out along the line, Fernandez's stomach grumbled. He glanced around, then sighed. "Shit ain't exploding yet, so we might as well eat some chow." Jackie settled right into dishing up the food. Trays loaded, they moved to an isolated table, eating in silence. Fernandez surveyed the personnel coming and going from the cafeteria.

The word 'Administration' on a wall placard caught Crutchlow's eye. He followed its directions down two levels and then for a five-minute walk. Hands crammed in his pockets, he effused an attitude of nonchalant ubiquity—as if he's supposed to be here. Strolling along, he eavesdropped on conversations; his Mandarin wasn't half bad after six months in Mongolia. He picked up on Spanish discussions, another one of his learned languages. Most of the conversations were mundane: complaining and gossip. A few, though, alluded to problems in the complex stemming from a plane crash. Apparently, most of the security staff had perished in the accident.

Eventually, he arrived at the Administrative Unit while following a Hispanic man. He passed the double-door entrance, glancing over his shoulder. The man brushed his badge across a black square to the door's right.

CLICK

The man pulled one door open and ducked inside. Crutchlow abruptly about faced and caught the door before it closed. Peeking through the gap, a wide open room lay on the other side with dozens of people in cubicles. Some were pecking on typewriters while others perused documents, contemplative pencils poking at the corner of their mouths. A unit of China's Fifty-cent Army. Crutchlow considered going inside. He heard scuffling in the corridor. He let go of the door, spinning away as if he was leaving. Hands jammed into his pockets, he headed away from the sound.

Things usually start at the bottom. That's how Moreland saw it. He found a stairwell and entered. It went four levels down. *There's no telling if this place is a block of rooms or a spread-out network of random tunnels. I better watch my trail, so I don't get lost.* He exited at the bottom into a long corridor that angled left. It was devoid of people. His footsteps echoed loudly. Steeling along, he came to a metal door painted blue with a brass handle. He tugged it open. Inside, it was dark and humid. Moreland groped for a light switch, found one, and flicked it on. LED lights running a hundred meters away illuminated an Olympic-sized pool of water.

A swimming pool? No. A cistern. They've got enough water for—months? He switched off the lights and exited. Further along, he found three more such potable water stores. The next level up was dry goods storage. People coming and going through a Dutch door. A sign above the door read, 'Supply Unit.' Not wanting to draw attention, he passed through the area without pausing. On his way back, he ran into Crutchlow, entering a stairwell.

They huddled inside.

"Seen anything interesting?" Crutchlow asked, leaning over a railing, scanning below.

Peering up the stairwell, Moreland said, "I found a huge set of cisterns on the fourth level, supplies and warehouse on the third. How about you?"

"Administration. The office people. And I mean a massive office full of people. Looked like a Fifty-cent Army op."

"The disinformation squad?" He scratched at his cheek. "That'd make sense. We'll note it. Ready to head back?"

"Yeah," Crutchlow said, nodding. "Let's go."

They found Perkins and Roberts rearranging the bodies in a single crate. With the extra help, they soon had all four corpses hidden inside it. Moreland dragged a pallet jack over and rammed it under the crate. He pumped it off the ground and said, "Ready to roll."

"Let's talk a minute," Perkins said as he washed his hands at a nearby sink. The others gathered round. Perkins tore off some paper towel and backed away from the sink. "What did you guys find? I've got a place for us to set up shop. With beds even."

Roberts said, "I found the medical unit. Looks well stocked and up-to-date. I couldn't get a better look, though. They wouldn't let me come inside." He wadded up a paper towel, tossing it at the garbage can for a three pointer.

"They've got months of stored water," Moreland said. "Down in the basement, there's at least four Olympic pool-sized cisterns filled to the brim. Next floor up is warehousing and supplies."

Perkins grunted, sawing at his chin, eyes going to Crutchlow.

"I followed the signs to the Administration Unit. Lots of cubicles, and dozens of people using old typewriters, but no computers. My guess is a Fifty-cent Army disinformation unit." He raised his eyebrows and shrugged.

"Alright," Perkins said, "All good stuff." He glared down at the crate. "Let's get this over with--."

"Hey, Perk, I also found a place in the main cavern where we can toss these guys." Roberts jabbed a thumb at the crate. "I spotted an oil drum corral where they're storing the empty lube containers. It looked secluded enough that we could pack these guys up without being seen."

"Well," Perkins said, stepping toward the door, "lead the way. You three haul the bodies up. I'll stay here with her." He pointed his chin at Lucy.

"Over there." Roberts pointed to a berm on the tarmac's edge.

"Man," Moreland said. "That's a long way."

Crutchlow pushed the crate from behind. "Then let's get moving!"

They hustled across the open area, not stopping until safely behind the berm. Dozens of empty oil drums arranged neatly. After confirming they were alone, Moreland pried off a barrel top, found it empty, and waved the others over. Crutchlow and Roberts opened the crate and dragged out a body.

"Aw, man," Roberts said, "they're getting stiff. Gross!"

Crutchlow grimaced and held his breath. Ten minutes later, they slapped the lid on the last barrel.

"Halt!"

The CIA team froze. Behind them, a lone guard stepped out of the shadows.

VII

At the end of a long day, Yimu Fang typically retired to his private quarters. The old-school nature of this operation forced him to write his reports by hand. There was no computer in his room. The studio apartment afforded him the basics. In the studio space, his desk, bookshelves, bed, and filing cabinets took up one wall. On the far wall, a skinny closet and dresser. His kitchen was an alcove across from his desk. Opposite the bed, a lavatory with shower.

Still in uniform, Fang lay on the bed. He flipped through movies on the facility's internal entertainment system. It wasn't internet connected. The media streamed from several servers in the Central Information Technology Unit. Another disconnect with the outside world. He lifted a cigarette butt to his mouth and took one last drag before crushing it out in the ashtray on his nightstand.

Knuckles rapped lightly on the door.

"Come in!"

The doorknob turned. Then it cracked open. An Asian teen poked her head through the crack.

Fang eyed her. "Oh, hello." He rose from the bed, hand extended. "Come in, come in."

The woman slipped inside and closed the door noiselessly. She demurely bowed at Fang. "Good evening, Commander Fang."

Fang stepped close, gently reaching a hand up, dragging it through her black hair. He smiled and looked into her eyes. "You are so beautiful. What is your name?"

The woman smiled weakly, hands folded in front. "Lei Ning."

Fang put an arm across her shoulders and guided her to the bed. "Join me, Lei." He patted the mattress.

Lei removed her silken robe, revealing her naked body. A wolfish grin spread across his face. He stepped close, then kissed her on the shoulder and caressed it. He backed away, and she climbed onto the bed, lying on her side facing him. Fang, still dressed in his black military fatigues with boots off, removed his outer shirt, revealing a white tank top. He undid his belt, dropping his pants where he stood. Though glad for her presence, something distracted Fang.

The female CIA officer will not be pliable like this girl. She wouldn't give it up without a fight. Fang lay back on the bed. Lei sidled up next to him, caressing his torso and resting her head on his shoulder. *Violating her would be very—exciting. But perhaps unproductive. No, I'll save that for when she breaks as a reward.*

He chuckled.

"What is it, Commander?" Lei asked, lifting her head to meet his eyes. "What is funny? Did I do som--"

Fang smiled at her, running a hand through her hair. "No. Not you. Something else. Don't worry about it."

She resumed rubbing his chest.

The isolation and quarantine of the complex meant no higher ups around at this hour. Questions and investigations were eventually coming about the downed airplane. Half the Communist Chinese Party's plan had gone down in flames at that unfortunate event. The plague was supposed to make subjugating the world easy. Things are complicated now. China must stoke flames of fear at maximum for the rest of their plan to work. Already, disinformation social media posts were being authored. Scheduled for release—when the time was right.

As head of security at the facility, Fang was understaffed. The plane crash completely wiped out the German contingent of foreign mercenaries that he had been counting on. They weren't even there twenty-four hours before Gruben and his team had downed the aircraft. Now he had a handful of security personnel. Until more got inducted and trained. Fang drew a deep breath, exhaling slowly.

Lei sat up, slid close, and began rubbing his scalp. "Let your troubles go."

Fang closed his eyes, but his mind refused to let go. *At least, the corona virus, made it to Wuhan.*

A different shipment was still traveling to Africa, targeting football matches and population centers. Not as lethal as the Bubonic plague, but fully capable of instilling mass fear and chaos. It would've been the third, last wave. Now it must suffice as the second and final wave. The one that ends Western economic domination. This was a highly guarded state secret. Only the top three CCP leaders knew of the project. Secret lab notwithstanding.

Fang knew because he had access to a lot of confidential information others did not. His Ministry of State Security job required it. He'd slowly pieced it all together. But those scientists got liquidated weeks ago. Their memory wiped from the Earth's history. In Wuhan, the Military World Games made a convenient target. The first batch released successfully. World-wide spread of the weaponized corona virus happened overnight when hundreds of foreign competitors returned home infected.

"Turn over. I rub your back."

Fang obliged, rolling onto his stomach, arms folded under his chin. *Amazingly, somehow, Xiang Peng had kept these projects a secret.* The Chinese president, Xiang Peng, and the highest leadership under him, already fully immunized for both pathogens, had retreated to remote island compounds and underground bunkers in the desert. *Yet, I noticed none of them were here. Everything they need is here, but they aren't. He frowned a moment. Then sighed. Well, of course, the first Bubonic weapon getting neutralized changed things.*

Thankfully, the overall plan remained the same. Peng and the others fell back on plan 'A'. The one everybody else in the anti-West cabal thought was the only plan of initial attack. They had spent the last few decades escalating a war against the west. Surreptitiously undermining their culture on the internet, in universities, world bodies, world finance, and world commerce. Against personal freedom and individual liberty. Against hedonism. Through demoralization, disruption, and division, the Chinese chiseled away at the city on the hill's foundations.

Armies got assembled, not on battlefields, but in cubicle farms and call centers. The Fifty-cent Army. 'Soldiers' maintained one hundred fake identities each as internet trolls with online fake accounts, news producers, influencers, and general disinformation. The psychological warfare grew steadily, but the Chinese out-stripped the world with its manpower capability. They could sway almost any public opinion in whatever direction benefited China.

Fang moaned as Lei worked out the kinks of his tired, sinewy body.

I'm perfectly happy with the way things turned out. Except my lack of enough security people.

Fang closed his eyes and tried not to think about the secret that he, as the Unit 57 Head of Security, and Ministry of State Security Officer was keeping: that they had no security team. It currently comprised Fang, four subordinates, and a few mercenary types. *If one of these mercenaries finds out the truth, it will force us into a hasty exit. Those thugs won't loaf around here for long without a strong security force.*

Plan 'B' roped in disaffected, actionable young people across all nationalities for use during and after the bio-weapons ran their course. Neo-Nazis, Yakuza, MS13, and several other lesser known underworld mercenaries. They would return to the world as ready-made Stasi. They could fit in better than Chinese people in predominantly Asian, Caucasian, or Hispanic regions.

Now they're in limbo, while things re-calibrate. Orders from on high told the facility Commander to hold down the fort, occupying the foreign recruits with internet troll duties and whatever busy work they could come up with. They kept them happy with allotments of booze, weed, and decent food. Command also saw fit to provide a cadre of good-time girls. Fang and Chen, the facility commander, got first dibs on women flown in. Before the plane got destroyed, the pair kept a private harem to themselves. All the other women prostituted themselves among the personnel, pulling double duty as whores and, Fang feared, as spies.

In this war of attrition, Fang felt fortunate he was here. Cutoff from the world. Safe from all plagues. His parents and brother lived in the world. Although he thought of them occasionally, they would never hinder his duty. Even if it meant them dying. *How many will perish? How empty will the world become? How are they so confident? I guess they're not so in control if one Mossad man can thwart them. China can beat any country in a war of attrition. We've plenty of fat for trimming with all those mouths to feed. Cannon fodder.* Zombie movies he had watched scratched and moaned at the back of his mind. *What if this facility became the last outpost of humanity?*

Fang rolled onto his back. A smile split his face as he took in Lei's naked breasts.

I'd be okay.

The CIA and Mossad showing up like they did bothered him. It was like he'd forgotten to lock the front door before leaving the house. Drone patrols had missed them. They easily hijacked a truck. Granted, highly trained agents wouldn't find that difficult. He'd be wise not to underestimate them. Despite that, they should never have gotten into a position to destroy that aircraft. Fortunately, Gruben and the others were completely under his control. He had all the time in the world.

Lei slid her hand down into his underwear. He groaned. *We'll start recruiting from the facility personnel tomorrow for a new security team. And those agents*—He groaned again.

I   don't   care   right   now.

VIII

The CIA team collectively thought the same question: did this guy see them loading bodies in barrels? If he had, he's brave to approach alone. On the other hand, maybe he hadn't seen the corpses. Perkins rubbed his palms on pant legs and took a step toward the man. Movement behind the lone soldier caught Perkin's eye. A silhouette trotted up behind the guard.

QWANG!

The guard winced with crossed eyes, then crumpled into a heap. Fernandez stepped from the shadows, a toothy grin glowing white, shovel in hand. Jackie, wearing a face of concern, followed, eyes pegging on the downed guard. It wasn't out of compassion rather a lost chance at getting a message out. He shook his head and hurried to the others.

"Hey, guys! Fancy meeting you here."

Yellow helmet in one hand, the other plowing his hair, Moreland said, "Oh, man, I thought it was all over just now!" He strode over and clasped hands with Fernandez. The others followed suit, all smiles and relief. When one of the pack was missing in action, then found, it was a massive relief.

Crutchlow asked, "You okay? We were worried about you."

"Aw, I didn't know you cared," Fernandez said with a chuckle. Moreland reached up and gave his head a playful shove, eliciting laughter all around. In slow motion, Fernandez swung a roundhouse kick at Moreland's head. Balanced on one leg, he said, "Me and old Jackie here, we been looking for you dudes, too." Biting his lower lip, he pantomimed knocking Moreland's head off. Abruptly, he lowered his leg and dropped the stance. "Are you hungry? I know where we can get food."

Roberts, reminded he hadn't eaten, said, "Seriously?" He scratched at the back of his neck. "I guess that makes sense. We should pack up this guy, though. I wanna get out of here, get back to the workshop."

"Roger that," Crutchlow said, as he selected another empty barrel. "This one will do."

Perkins and Lucy hid in the shadows outside the workshop. He knew the others would return soon. When Perkins saw them, he emerged from the darkened alcove, Lucy in tow, clutched at the elbow. The hallways and corridors weren't lit like a hospital. Overhead lights were ten meters apart. Plenty of light for movement. And shaded areas for hiding. "Hey," Perkins said, raising his free hand.

Moreland and the others halted, tension rippling through them like a shockwave.

"Fuck." Crutchlow said. "You okay? You scared the shit outta me."

"We're good." He glanced at Lucy, who was staring behind them. "That supervisor came back to the workshop. So, we sneaked out before he saw——."

Fernandez stepped from behind the stoic Roberts.

"Fern? Awesome!" They clasped hands, exchanging a quick bro hug. "And Jackie? Glad you guys fared okay."

"And didn't get discovered," Fernandez said with a wink and finger gun aimed at Perkins, who grinned.

Smiles spread across Jackie and Lucy's faces. Perkins permitted them a quick hug, then they separated but continued holding hands. The Americans had them in a serious pickle. Enough time had gone by without them sounding the alarm that investigators would suspect them of being traitors.

Moreland and Roberts took a step toward the shop.

"Wait," Perkins said. "Follow me. We'll come back later for our gear. Let's get a base of operations set up first."

Moreland and Roberts exchanged a glance, shrugged, and fell in behind the others, already moving out with Perkins. "I hope its luxury suites. I'm not sleeping on no damn floor," Moreland said.

A few minutes later, five infiltrators, a head taller than their two hostages, stood awkwardly close, assessing a quad's amenities. They shuffled around each other, taking it in, nervous about being trapped in the tiny space.

After a round of bathroom breaks, Perkins called a huddle.

"You said you know where we can get food?"

Fernandez stepped close, resting an elbow on a bunk bed. "Yeah, there's a cafeteria. We just walked in, got some food and chowed down."

"Thanks, you fuck!" Crutchlow groused, hands going to hips. "While we were killing those guys, you were killing a burger?"

"Hey, man, I didn't know. Shiiiit. I figured it would be good intel, and we were blending in. So, fuck you."

Crutchlow grunted. "Well, where is the place? I'm starving."

Moreland scratched the back of his head. "Are we sure it's safe to eat?"

All eyes flicked to Fernandez. His eyebrows shot up. "So far," hand going to his belly, "I feel fine." He grinned like a Cheshire cat. Being the newest member on the team, he couldn't do anything right. It irked the others he'd done well on his own. Naturally, it turned into something else to bust his new balls about.

"Alright, we'll consider him our canary in the coal mine then," Perkins said. "Fernandez, you take Crutchlow, since he's the hangriest, and get him fed."

Roberts, lying on a bottom bunk, hands behind his head, said, "Bring back a little extra." He jutted his chin at Jackie and Lucy, sitting side-by-side on the opposite bunk bed. "Unless you wanna take them, too?"

"No," Perkins said, standing and grasping the doorknob. "They'll stay here. And don't bring back a little. Bring back as much as you can without drawing suspicion." He cracked the door and peered out. "Looks clear. Be careful. Oh, and test your radio with two clicks when you get there. Can the radios reach that far? We're under a lot of rock. Give it a try."

"We'll test it." Fernandez and Crutchlow slipped out.

An hour later, the entire team and hostages had food in their stomachs. Tension waned, and they rested for a time, recounting their observations. Perkins had stuffed Jackie and Lucy into the toilet closet while they spoke. Their silence didn't instill trust as he felt they were listening keenly. It was the quick looks away that told him they were paying attention.

Crutchlow's discovery of the admin unit appealed the most. "What we should do," Perkins said, scratching at a cheek, "is get into that admin area."

"I was thinking of something a little more—in-depth," Crutchlow said.

Perkins, cocking an eyebrow, said, "What do you mean?"

"I mean, we work there. Whatever happened to the security team threw a major monkey wrench into--," Crutchlow's eyes scanned the room, "into whatever this place is for. Anyway, maybe we can get a man on the inside during this confusion."

"Not a bad idea," Perkins said, stroking his chin. "You say you heard them talking about a staffing shortage? Wonder what would happen if you showed up and just said, 'I'm the new guy?'"

"It's worth a try," Crutchlow said with a shrug. "If they get suspicious, I'll just bail."

I've only got a month left! Perkins clenched his jaw. Through gritted teeth, he said, "How did I get mixed up in this bullshit? In less than thirty days, I'll be retired." He rubbed his face with both hands.

Crutchlow heaved a sigh. "I know, man. We gotta do what we gotta do." He patted Perkin's shoulder. "Cheer up, you'll end up with a sweet medal after this."

"Probably not since it's a classified mission," Moreland said, curling a corner of his mouth.

Perkins shot a glare at Moreland, who put his hands up. "Hey, just say'n, don't get your hopes set on a medal."

Perkins snorted. "I already got my share of medals. They can keep 'em. Alright. Crutchlow. Moreland. In the morning, you two go see about getting 'jobs' or something. For now, we lie low, and get some rest until morning. I'll take the first watch until," he glanced at his wristwatch, "its twenty-two hundred now. So, at midnight, I get the next guy up."

Crutchlow, Moreland, and Fernandez hopped into beds, leaving a single bottom bunk open. As Roberts went to lie on it, Perkins said, "Let out Jackie and Lucy. And give them that bed."

Roberts frowned, striding over to the restroom and snatching the door open. He waved them out. "Come on." He pointed at the empty bed. Jackie and Lucy shuffled to it. They laid side-by-side, eyes on Roberts hovering over them.

Roberts spun around and slapped Fernandez on the thigh. "Move over, man. We gotta share."

Fernandez clucked his tongue, begrudgingly moving aside.

Perkins took a seat at a desk near the door. He rifled through the drawers and found a half done crossword puzzle booklet and ball-point pen. With a shrug, he whiled away the time solving the puzzles.

IX

Crutchlow and Moreland raided the laundry room down the hall. A dryer, conveniently unattended, had khaki pants and white button-down shirts more suited to office work rather than their blue coveralls or black fatigues. They stole what they needed and hustled back to the quad, changing into their new outfits while the others cycled through breakfast runs.

Dressed and ready, the infiltrators stood before their leader. Perkins looked the agents over, scrutinizing them like children on their first day of school.

Moreland, tugging at his groin, said, "Man, I feel like an idiot in this nerd get up. This is some private school uniform bullshit."

Perkins arched an eyebrow at the incongruous combat boots Moreland wore. "Your lace is untied. Make sure you hide those bogus badges after you get there."

Crutchlow peered down at his outfit. "There weren't any metro-man shoes handy. We look about like the others I saw in there yesterday."

"Alright," Perkins said, nodding, "I'll tail you there, in case something goes wrong." He turned to Roberts. "I'll come back when it looks like they're safe inside."

"Roger that," Roberts said, eyeing Jackie and Lucy lying on their bunk bed. Jackie met his eyes. "I hope Fern brings some fruit back."

Jackie perked up. "Yes. Fruit. Please."

"You ready?" Crutchlow asked, turning to Moreland, who was tying his boot.

He cinched his laces with a frown and said, "Yeah, let's move out."

Perkins followed a discrete few meters behind. The Administrative Unit door, propped open with a floor wedge, had a clearly marked sign attached in multiple languages. This was a high traffic area. Every department had contact with the Administration Unit. Inside, a young Hispanic man sat at a front desk, sorting papers. He wasn't surprised at all to see Crutchlow approaching. Perkins observed from the hallway. *Looks like business as usual.* After a brief exchange, the receptionist turned, pointing somewhere further in the work center. Moreland gave a surreptitious hand signal to Perkins that everything was okay, so he broke off and returned to the quad.

The CIA operators said they'd lost their paperwork in transit. They couldn't remember who, but someone directed them here for work and new identification badges. The receptionist advised Crutchlow that the supervisor would need to approve fresh papers. He directed them to her office.

Moreland and Crutchlow followed the instructions, stopping at the supervisor's door and peeking inside. A chubby, bespectacled woman hunched over her desk, perusing paperwork—Long Su. Crutchlow knocked on the door frame. Su glanced up, eyebrows knitting.

"Yes, what is it?" Her impatient demeanor reassured the CIA men. She wasn't likely to bother with details like where, exactly, they came or their documentation.

Hands clasped in front, Crutchlow and Moreland sidled into the office, standing before the woman's desk. "Work we here," Crutchlow said in wretched Mongol.

Su, leaning back in her plastic office chair, grimaced. "Oh damn, your Mongol is painful."

In Spanish, Moreland asked, *"Habla espanol?"*

Su scowled. "What is that? Spanish? I don't speak Spanish. Do you know English? You look like Englishmen."

Crutchlow blew out a breath. "Yes, thank God you know English."

Su smiled and spread her arms. "Finally, we can get this over with. As you can see, I'm busy." She rested elbows on the chair's arms, fingers forming a steeple.

Moreland and Crutchlow exchanged a glance. Crutchlow spread a hand on his chest. "Somebody lost our paperwork."

"They're looking for it," Moreland said.

"Yeah. We don't know where to go. And we heard they needed help here." Crutchlow half-smiled with a shrugged. Their cocky gamble suddenly not such a good idea.

A frown curved Su's mouth while she tapped her fingers together. She looked both men up and down, pulling in a deep breath, and sighed. "That should be fine. Your English fluency will help in translation." Su reached down and pulled a desk drawer open. She fished around inside and brought out two temporary identification badges. "Here, take these to Xuan Lingxin." The portly supervisor leaned forward, arm extended with the badges.

Crutchlow and Moreland each took one.

"Tell her you're new here and need occupational duties." She nodded curtly, snatching up a pen. Moreland and Crutchlow bowed and exited her office.

The CIA men examined their badges with wolfish grins as they clipped them to a lapel. "Man," Moreland said, "I can't believe we just walked in and got handed some badges."

Crutchlow, shaking his head, said, "Yeah, I know. Almost too easy." He gave a furtive glance around the enormous cubicle farm. Dozens of heads bobbed above the low cubicle walls. Typewriters clacked and papers shuffled. It reminded Crutchlow of the press room in a major newspaper in decades past. "Let's find this Lingxin dudette."

A man they queried in the closest cubicle directed them further back. A plain office door stood open on the right. They strode to the door and peered inside. A slender, gray-haired, Chinese woman sat at a desk, scrutinizing reports. Her eyes flicked up, glaring over the black rims of her reading glasses. "What do you want?"

Crutchlow cleared his throat. In English, he said, "We're new and need occupations." He pointed toward Su's office. "We just spoke with Su. She directed us to you."

Lingxin frowned. "Do you speak Mandarin? Russian? Something other than English?"

"We're both fluent in English, Spanish, and some Mongol."

Lingxin sucked at her teeth. "Okay. We will find something for you." She spied their temporary badges. "First thing, you'll need permanent ID badges." Lingxin pointed to the right. "Go further down this wall. There's an open room. Wait there until I get someone to come take your pictures and make badges."

"Yes, ma'am. Thank you."

Her eyes narrowed then she waved dismissively and plucked the receiver off a beige phone.

Arriving at the darkened room, Moreland leaned in and switched on the overhead light. The three meter by three meter room contained a tripod-mounted camera aimed at the wall. A folding table sat to the right. Atop the table sat a lamination machine. Stacks of clear plastic ID laminate were stacked next to ID paper. Crutchlow surreptitiously pocketed a few plastic covers and papers. Moreland watched the door. Stepping close, Crutchlow said, "Got us some extras. Might come in handy later."

A slender Asian man rose from a cubicle nearby, corded phone pressed to his ear. He turned, searching. He spotted the CIA men, hung up, then hurried over to them. In Mandarin, he said, "I'm here to make your identification."

"I think he's here to make the ID's," Crutchlow said.

Moreland nodded agreement.

Pantomiming what he needed, the man had each person stand against the wall. Not knowing their information, he handed the ID paper over, gesturing at them to fill in the blanks. They complied, carefully watching everything the man did. Ten minutes later, they had official Unit 57 badges.

Lingxin took them to their new occupations. Crutchlow got dropped off at a mail room, sorting packages. Moreland went to a vault filled with paper stacks and hundreds of filing cabinets.

Though taught Mandarin in a six-month crash course a year ago, both men were rusty, having not used the language much while stationed in Mongolia. Mongol was what they spoke most often. Fortunately, as Crutchlow got instructed on mail sorting, the language began coming back to him. The characters on paper were easier to decipher than spoken words. He was to sort letters and packages for distribution throughout the complex. Left to his devices, he shrugged. "Well, might as well get to work."

They led Moreland to a different section of the Admin unit. A dozen boxes, filled with paper stuffed folders, were on this room's floor. "These folders must be destroyed." The man pointed at an industrial-sized shredder in the corner. "Shred everything. Even the folders they come inside."

Moreland chewed at the corner of his mouth, hands on hips. "Okay."

The man gave a curt nod, spun around and departed.

Two hours later, Moreland hadn't shredded a thing. Rifling through the folders, he uncovered dossiers of people on the crashed airplane. They had all come from Germany. All young men under the age of twenty-five. Black and white photos, paper clipped to each folder, identified whose information it contained. He recognized one man: Herman Baader. Perusing Baader's file, he found a line drawing of the facility. "This might come in handy." He slid the map into a sock and resumed reading.

A speaker embedded in the ceiling screeched with feedback, then several *dings,* like a tiny triangle being tapped. Curious, Moreland moved to the room's entryway. Peering out, he saw the entire cubicle herd leaving their desks. As a man passed him, Moreland tried some Mandarin. "Leave everybody?"

The man glared at Moreland but said nothing and kept walking. A man trailing behind said, "Time to eat. Aren't you hungry?"

"Oh, okay. Yeah," Moreland replied, eyes scanning for Crutchlow, who emerged from the mailroom with several other workers. They made eye contact. Crutchlow broke off from the herd. The two of them slowed down while the rest hurried onward.

"What do they got you doing?" Moreland asked.

"Mail room duty," Crutchlow said with a shrug. "I'm seeing lots of messages referencing a bio-weapon."

Nodding, Moreland said, "Yeah, they've got me running the Ollie North machine. I've seen papers talking about a security unit. They all died in that plane crash with that Baader dude Perk was after. They were escorting a bio-weapon to Beijing, but it crashed right after takeoff. There is something else happening in Italy and Africa. Wasn't much detail on those ops."

Crutchlow, scratching at his neck, said, "I wonder what happened with that?"

"All I know is everything I'm seeing is referencing a virus. It's already released in some place called Wuhan. What the fuck, dude? Is China starting the apocalypse?"

Moreland bit at his lip. Both men's thoughts went straight to their wives and children back home.

Crutchlow eyed the ceiling. "I think this place is a quarantine zone or something. That would explain its remoteness. No bug is gonna survive out here."

Moreland grabbed Crutchlow's forearm. "We gotta get a message out."

Eyes wide, Crutchlow nodded rapidly. By now, the Admin section was a ghost town. Every person had left for lunch. The CIA men searched high and low for a telephone with an outside line. Even a ham radio would do. Desk phones only got used for internal communication, having no outside line. None had access to an outside line. Inside Su's unlocked office, they searched everywhere. A shiny red phone in a desk drawer looked promising.

Crutchlow, hoping he didn't need a password, picked up the receiver. He rolled his eyes with relief and sighed. Glancing at Moreland, he said, "I've got a dial tone." He punched in memorized digits to a 'hello' number.

A woman answered, all folksy and kind. "Hello, Bluntville Office Supplies."

"We couldn't get inside our copy machine, but we figured it out. No need for a service technician right now." He eyed Moreland, keeping watch at the door. "There was a bug in it, but it left the building. We'll let you know if we see any more."

"Okay, sir. Glad to hear all is well. Call us if you have any further problems."

Crutchlow dropped the phone back on its cradle, crossing his fingers that someone did not monitor the line in real time. The brief, coded exchange told Langley they were okay and they'd come across a bio-weapon."

"We need to tell them about this plague coming." A murmur outside grew louder. "They're coming back. Come on, let's get outta here."

At 5:00 p.m., another chime sounded on the PA. All the office workers dropped what they were doing and left. Moreland and Crutchlow followed suit. Some went to the cafeteria, while others returned to the barracks unit. The pair ate with the rest of workers, pocketing a few small boxes of raisin bran, returning to relieve Perkins and Fernandez at the quad for chow. Jackie and Lucy got dry cereal for dinner. The dark specter of an evil plot loomed over their heads when they told the others about a bio-weapon on the loose.

X

Head fuzzy. Dim light. Shadows undulating. A voice, distant, muffled. Reality whooshed back into Karl. *I'm in the interrogation room. Again.*

Movement behind. "Good, you're awake. Today, let's talk about the CIA woman, Chi-Hye."

Karl lifted his head. *How does he know her name?*

"Tell me about this Tonya Chi-Hye. What does she do? Why is she working with the Mossad?"

"She doesn't--," Karl winced. Just like that, by implication, he acknowledged Tonya Chi-Hye's identity.

"Don't lie to me. Wake up!"

Karl squeezed his eyes shut, then opened them wide.

WHACK!

Karl cringed in his chair, arms cuffed behind, stinging pain radiating from his shoulder.

"Wake up! Why is CIA operative with you?"

Not sure what he'd divulged a few minutes ago, Karl said, "CIA? What are? You--."

THWACK!

"I ask the goddamn questions! Now, answer me."

I'm going to beat him senseless with that baton. One of these sessions... I just need to avoid that sedative.

He'd noticed they didn't put the sedative deep. A bubble formed under his skin, bulging for a moment, a chemical droplet seeping out. He'd considered squeezing the spot like a zit, but felt that might actually spread the fluid further.

If I can suck it out before they take me, maybe I'll have a fighting chance in here. If ingesting it doesn't still sedate me. Or kill me. If I'm quick, though, I can spit it out. Under my mattress or somewhere.

The trail of Karl's thoughts ended there. Day after day, sedated and interrogated, his memory and goals had nebulized. He could begin the fantasy of escape, but his thoughts rarely went beyond escaping. What to do afterward was too much to contemplate.

Avoid sedation to live or die attempting an escape? Does it even matter? If I can kill myself, I... Suicide. Truly envisioning a scenario where you do it like a reflex. That gave him pause. *I don't know if I could just end my life. I'd rather do it myself than let them have the pleasure. More importantly, they won't get any more intel from me. They're just going to liquidate me, eventually.*

THWACK THWACK

"You're not answering," Fang said, singsong style. The man paced behind Karl, occasionally kicking a flashlight on the floor so its beam passed randomly through Karl's chair legs. The strobe of shadows splayed across the wall in front of him. "What are you thinking about, Gruben? Escape? Your friends? Home? Suicide? There won't be a home soon, you know. And we're aware of suicide attempts."

Karl dared to glance behind. "What are you--," he said, cutting himself off for asking a question. He braced and said, "Israel won't go away. Not so quick. They'd nuke the Arabs first."

Fang chuckled. "Yes—prisoner—tell me all about what's been going on. The Arabs? Ha! They're puppets too. We already spread a virus across the world. People are dying. Do you know why?" He kicked the flashlight, sending the shadows into a maelstrom.

Karl turned left and right, finally shrugging. "You communist bastards are insane. Why would--?"

THWACK!

That one struck his hands. Karl sucked in air through gritted teeth, fingers throbbing. He pulled with all his might on the restraints. *Come on! Break! Let me at this motherfucker!* After a few seconds he tired, relaxing to a slump, head hanging. Saliva dripping from his mouth, Karl said, "Please. Stop. Please stop hitting me!" He screamed 'me' at the top of his lungs. It was the most sincere thing he'd ever uttered.

A hand touched on each shoulder. Karl flinched. "Okay," Fang intoned. "Then give me information. It really is that easy. Help us help you."

It was beyond tempting. The offer nearly brought Karl to tears. He couldn't give up. They wouldn't let him. As long as he was alive and in their control, all he could do was fight back in his mind. *Maybe we're all giving them enough disinformation. They'll figure nothing out. We would all be stalling, lying, and plotting. We would remember our training. I have to believe that.* "Tonya," Karl bit at his lip and heaved a deep breath. "She's not really CIA."

Fang chuckled. "Gruben, Gruben, Gruben. She's already admitted as much and signed a confession. Your German agent friends Arnold and Kevin have corroborated her story. You really shouldn't try to lie in your condition. I can tell."

Karl furrowed his forehead. *German agents?* A tiny glimmer of hope buoyed him. *I love you guys! You're still fighting and giving them bullshit. Unless he's trying to trip me up. Shit. It's something, at least.*

Hours later, the heavy steel door slammed on Karl's cell, jolting him awake. A moment of confusion and panic shook him before he oriented himself. Prostrate on his stomach, he dropped his head back onto the prison bed. *It's over for now.* His stomach rumbled noisily. Fully awake, Karl rolled onto his back. There concrete was, unchanged. He massaged his wrists and fingered the injection site on his forearm. It still had a vague welt. Bringing it to his mouth, he sucked on the tiny hole. *Blood and something bitter. It's the sedative residue.* He gazed forlornly at the door. *What would I do if I escaped? Where would I go?*

Karl lay on the bed until he fell asleep, too worn out for exercise. Slumber was his only escape. A welcome retreat from this reality. Until the nightmares began. Then it was toss and turn until mealtime or an interrogation. *Would they even send help? This is much bigger than following a gang of thugs. Is it politically possible? China can't be acting alone.* The concept of plausible deniability pushed his brain over the edge of collapse. He got two hours of rest before a nightmare woke him. He'd seen the man's scalp tear again. Only this time, they shared a coffin.

XI

Time in the quad ticked by at half speed. Or so it seemed. Luckily, Roberts had the foresight to bring a deck of cards. Otherwise, they'd be climbing the walls in this small space by now. The isolation and tension were especially taxing on Jackie and Lucy. Confined to the bed or bathroom, they had been quiet and compliant until the boredom got to them. The MSS agent rose from the bunk with Lucy.

Perkins, Roberts, and Fernandez looked up from their card game on the opposite bunk.

With a dismissive wave, Jackie said, "I'm tired of sitting around. Just want to pace."

"Sit down." The growl in Perkin's voice gave Jackie pause.

"What? I'm fucking tired of just laying here."

"Too bad. Now, sit back down." Perkins stood up from sitting on the bunk and loomed over Jackie.

"How long you think you can keep this up? Being in here driving me crazy," Jackie said, folding his arms, refusing to budge.

Perkin's hands went to his hips. "Cry me a river. Yeah, none of us wanna be here. Sit back down or I'll—."

Lucy scooched closer to the bed's edge and tugged Jackie's elbow.

"Alright, alright," Jackie said, holding a placating hand up while jerking his other from Lucy's grasp. He shuffled to the bunk, stretched, scratched, eventually lowering his rear onto the bed. It made Perkins grin. They locked eyes, both men sizing up the other. He was a one hundred four kilogram warrior. Jackie barely weighed sixty kilos.

"You keep getting uppity and we'll bind your wrists. If you still won't behave, we'll gag you." Perkins folded his arms, glaring down at Jackie and Lucy. "There're all kinds of levels we can go." He pulled a hand out and snapped fingers. "Like that. We don't want to hurt you, but don't test me."

Lucy moved closer to Jackie, hugging his arm.

Perkins leaned forward slightly. "Got it?"

Jackie hesitated a moment, his pride grappling with his good sense. Not to mention his training endlessly sounding a klaxon. The Americans had them. Their only hope was keeping vigilant for an opportunity. He looked away, nodding. "Got it."

"Good." Perkins returned to the bunk, picking up his cards. He spread them in his hands and frowned.

"Your go," Fernandez said.

An hour later, the PA chimed, announcing the workday's end. Fifteen minutes passed before Moreland and Crutchlow returned. They put Jackie and Lucy in the bathroom again. Both received another small box of cereal for dinner.

"Well, they're not gonna have any problems taking a dump," Perkins said, folding his arms and leaning a shoulder against the bunk bed. "All that fiber they're eating." He shook his head. "How'd it go?"

Crutchlow exchanged a glance with Moreland. "Well, we got badged." He tapped the clear badge holder clipped to his lapel. Inside was a laminated ID with his picture on it.

Perkins leaned off the bunk, eyes squinting at the photo. "Nice. How'd you pull that off?" The CIA team sat across from each other on the bunk beds. Perkins remained on his feet, returning a shoulder to the bunk's edge.

Eyebrows up, Crutchlow said, "It was pretty damned easy, actually."

"Yeah," Moreland said, obviously excited about their success. "We just walked in, said they lost our shit and--."

"—and," Crutchlow interjected, "they're so busy and understaffed, the supervisor didn't make a big deal out of it. We're in like Flynn."

"What about the rest of us? Do you think we can get more badges? It would sure make things easier." Perkins eyed the others, who were nodding agreement.

"Shouldn't be a problem," Crutchlow said with a smirk. "The ID room is wide open. Anybody can walk in."

Perkins stroked at his chin. "Probably not the new guys, though. Someone might find it suspicious. We need to do it covertly."

Moreland said, "The entire office splits at lunch for half an hour. Which reminds me, we got a message out to HQ."

Perkin's eyebrows went up. "You did? Good. How? What did you say?"

"We found one outside line. It's a bat-phone stashed in a drawer." He looked at Moreland, who shrugged. "We called the 'hello' number, told 'em we're here and working on it."

"Yeah, and gave 'em a heads up on the bio-weapon."

Perkins sat next to Crutchlow, elbows on his knees, hands clasped. "That's good. We've got a time stamp, at least. What do you think the odds are we can use that phone regularly?"

"I dunno," Crutchlow said, rubbing his hands on thighs. "They hide it in the supervisor's desk. Like she was the only one allowed to use it."

Perkins nodded. "Or... that could mean she's doing something she's not supposed to by having it."

"Yeah, I suppose," Crutchlow said, then shook his head. "Never mind the phone." He elbowed Moreland. "We got intel on that bio-weapon."

Eyes widening, Moreland said, "Yeah, that Baader dude, he was in that grease smear of a plane crash. He and his entire crew were on it guarding a bio-weapon. Destination: Beijing."

Silence chilled the room. Everyone's gears turning. The mental math quickly added up to their friends and families out there. Unaware.

"A second bio-weapon went somewhere called Wuhan. There's a facility there. I don't know if they deployed it there or what. From what I've read, it was going there to be released."

Crutchlow said, "And there's something going on in Italy and Africa. I guess these guys didn't have a need-to-know about that one. Because there ain't much intel on either op."

Perkins sawed at his chin. "Their Belt and Road initiative has gotten them deep into Africa. Italy, though. I dunno what's up with that. Never worked there." Confirmation of FPE's dead leader gave him pause. "Wow, so Baader's dead. Wonder if Chi-Hye and the Mossad dudes had anything to do with it? Something made that plane go down. How in the hell an airplane gets in here——." He flicked his eyes at the ceiling. "And out—is beyond me."

Fernandez asked, "And the idea that this bio-weapon was heading for Beijing and Wuhan? How could they infect their own people? That's some fucked up shit."

"Seriously," Roberts said, shaking his head. "What is it with these commies? Their people are just numbers." He snorted. "I guess we're just numbers, too."

"I don't know. The Chinese aren't known for being transparent. It could be them. It could be them working with somebody else. The point is, we're on the inside and making some outstanding progress. Good job, you two. We need to get IDs for everybody. You said lunch is a good time?"

Crutchlow shrugged, curling a corner of his mouth. "Maybe. I'd rather break in at night when we know there won't be any interruptions or awkward questions."

"Alright. So, we break in tonight. Me, Roberts, and you will go first." He checked his watch. "At 21:00. When we get back, I'll send Fernandez."

The PA erupted with an alarm tone. All eyes shot up to the ceiling mounted speaker. "Attention. Attention. There are several personnel missing. All personnel report to your supervisor for verification. Attention. Attention. There are several--,"

"Damn," Perkins said, whacking his knee with the back of a hand. "They've noticed those guys we took out. We need those badges. This might be the opportunity we wanted."

Crutchlow jabbed Moreland with an elbow. "Come on. We need to check in."

Incredulous, Moreland said, "Man, we just got here." He growled and rose.

The only way to know who is missing was to take a quick census, a simple roll call. After mustering in the hangar, Crutchlow lingered, while Moreland hurried back to the quad. He led Perkins and Roberts to admin, picked the lock, and filed inside. Crutchlow took the long way back to Admin, joining the team as they opened the door.

Moments later, Perkins blinked his eyes after the camera's flash strobe flare. The tripod mounted Polaroid *whirred* and spat out a developing photo. Crutchlow snatched the square, waving it like a fan.

"Alright, when you get that one done, we'll head back and send Fernandez."

Crutchlow trimmed the picture using a punch that made a perfect rectangular ID photo. He assembled the paper backing, carefully aligning the picture and running it through the lamination machine. A minute later, it came out the other side, melted smooth. Crutchlow trimmed the edges with scissors, sliding it into a badge holder as he handed it to Perkins.

"Alright," Perkins said, turning to leave. "Stand by for Fern."

"Roger that." Crutchlow said with a thumb up.

Perkins, feeling legitimate with a badge clipped to his lapel, pushed the quad's door open, a big grin on his face. He'd chosen the name Winston Smith. An ironic nod to the author George Orwell. The scene inside wiped his smile away in a microsecond.

Moreland was lying on the floor, hands clasped around his head. Fernandez had his silenced pistol trained on Jackie and Lucy, who clung to each other on their bunk bed.

Perkins darted inside and closed the door, stooping to glare at their captives. "What the hell happened?"

Fernandez sneered. "Commie motherfuckers tried to jump us." He lunged forward and kicked the bed's frame. Jackie and Lucy pressed against the wall. "They knocked the shit outta Moreland with a can of beans." He glanced down at the fallen agent. "His bitch missed me, though." Fernandez lunged at the couple again. "Plan failed, huh, commie motherfuckers!"

Perkins laid a hand on Fernandez's shoulder. "Keep it down." Pointing to Moreland, he said, "Is he okay?"

Fernandez shrugged and rubbed a cheek on his shoulder. "I think so—I guess. I haven't been able to check on him. It just happened a minute ago."

Perkins kneeled. Moreland groaned when he gave him a gentle shake. "Hey, buddy. You okay?"

"I don't wanna go to school today, Mom," Moreland said with a groan and grimace.

A smile split Perkin's face. "He's good." Turning to Jackie and Lucy, the smile fell away. "I told you not to try anything." He rose, stepped toward a backpack, and brought out a plastic bag of black zip ties. Ten minutes later, Jackie and Lucy lay side-by-side on the bunk bed—bound and gagged.

Perkins, dusting his hands off, said, "Alright, Fern." He turned to Fernandez and looked him over. "Get yourself cleaned up and go see Crutch for your badge."

"Roger that."

XII

Fernandez, moving solo through the complex, followed a man and woman. Their route led most of the way. Fernandez kept back enough they didn't feel like he was eavesdropping. About the distance between the ceiling lights; ten meters. He froze in a shadowed intersection. Three black uniformed men twenty meters up the corridor. They stopped the pair walking ahead of him. He couldn't hear what they were saying. His gut told him they were a search party. *Probably investigating the missing people.* Fernandez took a right at the next intersection, vectoring away from the vicinity. The circuitous route added ten minutes to his trip back.

He knocked softly on the admin door, furtively glancing up and down the vacant corridor. A few seconds later, Crutchlow cracked the door open, one eye peeping out. "It's about time." He pulled the door wide.

Fernandez slipped inside, eyes darting around the room. "Are we alone?"

Crutchlow clapped a hand on Fernandez's shoulder. "Relax. We're cool." He noticed the welt on his head. "What happened to your head? Everybody's gone for the day." He panned an arm across the cubicle farm. "Follow me. ID room is over here."

"Dude, those commie shitheads got the drop on me and Moreland. They clocked him in the head with a can of beans." Crutchlow halted and faced Fernandez, brows knit.

"Well, you're here, so I guess their insurrection failed?"

Fernandez massaged the back of his head. "Yeah, I about killed the *pendejos*. Perk showed up before I rage killed them." He gestured move along. "They're secure now," he said with a grin.

Crutchlow led the way. "Damned tricky bastards. Those two might be more than they appear. I don't and won't trust 'em. Matter of fact, we should've iced them on the road."

"I'll fudge my report if you fudge yours."

Crutchlow sighed. "We'll see how things go and save fudging in case of emergency." He glanced at Fernandez, who nodded. Crutchlow gave a curt nod, then stopped at the ID room's door.

The cubicle farm emptiness should've reassured Fernandez. Instead, it made him feel like someone could be out there, hiding in the maze of human corrals. Listening, watching. He touched at the crusted blood on his head where the can nicked him. "You sure we're safe? They don't have cameras or a night shift?" He asked as they passed into the ID room.

"Nah," Crutchlow intoned, taking up a position behind the camera. He pointed at a piece of blue tape on the floor. "Stand against that wall with your toes on the tape." Fernandez obliged, straightening himself, touching at his close-cropped hair.

"Gimme a break. Nobody will care about your pic."

A grin on Fernandez's face showed teeth. "Can't help it. Gotta look good."

With an eye-roll, Crutchlow said, "Say cheese."

"Blow me."

Click The camera flashed.

"How long?"

As Crutchlow plucked the fresh picture from the camera, he said, "Just a few minutes." He eyed Fernandez. "I can't believe that little man and woman got the drop on you guys. What, were you sleeping?"

"Man, I don't know. They've obviously been waiting for a chance. Perkins was so pissed, he hog-tied them both and gagged 'em."

Hunched over the table, writing on Fernandez's ID, Crutchlow said, "Pancho Villa. That's your new name."

Fernandez scowled for a moment, thinking Crutchlow was being funny. Peering over his shoulder as he put the badge through the laminator, Fernandez saw Pancho Villa printed on the card. "You don't think that name might raise some eyebrows?"

Crutchlow shrugged. "Doubt it. I've noticed a ton of Hispanic guys and gals around here. Most are former gang members or something. Working in the Social Media unit. Looks like the Fifty-cent army hired some mercenaries. They ain't history buffs if you get my drift. Anyway, Perkins went with Winston Smith and Moreland with Frans. I'm Hans."

Fernandez snickered. "Nice. Hopefully, they don't get pumped up by Jackie and Lucy."

Crutchlow snickered. "Yeah. This'll be done in a sec. We'll split up afterward."

"Roger that," Fernandez said, folding his arms and taking up lookout by the entry. The freshly laminated ID dropped into the exit tray thirty seconds later. Crutchlow picked it out, handing it to Fernandez in a clear holder.

He clipped it on and said, "Now I'm official. Let's get out of here--."

The main door burst opened. Yimu Fang, director of security, stepped through. Crutchlow had seen the man's picture in a chain of command flow chart. Not to mention his name on all those files. This wasn't good. The CIA men slowed their pace, exchanging a glance. "Act cool. That guy is head of security." They swallowed hard and proceeded.

Fang eyed them as they converged. Assuming they spoke English, he said, "Where is Su? I need her to confirm some identification badges."

Crutchlow and Moreland briefly glanced at each other, both aware their badges had no back-up paperwork within the system yet. Uncertain of their next move, Crutchlow put on a professional, can-do attitude. With a German accent, he said, "He is gone for the day, sir."

Fang eyed both men up and down. "You sound like one of Baader's people."

Crutchlow shrugged and smiled. "Baader?"

Fang grunted. "Never mind. Can you take care of it?" he said, handing over several badges.

Crutchlow accepted the ID's, sifting through them idly, taking a deep breath when he realized these were not copies of their bogus badges but of other individuals altogether. "Yah. Do you just need verification?"

Fang, peering around the cubicles, said, "Yes. These individuals recently arrived. I want to make sure they're who they say they are."

"If you'll follow me over zee records, I can get that information for you."

"You can?" Fernandez said.

Crutchlow elbowed him. "Yah, I'm qualified." He turned to Fang. "This way, Commander Fang."

The pair moved away. Fernandez made for the door. Crutchlow didn't realize Fernandez had bailed until he heard the door shut. *Better if I handle this alone, anyway.*

"You work late," Fang said, hands going behind his back.

"Yah, it's been crazy," he gestured, "what with zee plane crash and all."

"Yes. A very unfortunate event."

"I was just catching up on some sings."

For the next twenty minutes, Crutchlow pulled the individual's records. The Security Chief flipped through the file folders while Crutchlow digested the growing idea this man might know what happened to Chi-Hye and the Mossad guys. Part of him didn't enjoy helping the commie. Part of him said he should cut this guy's throat. Another part couldn't think of a casual way to inquire about the missing agents.

Fang, apparently satisfied, abruptly collected the ID's. "That will do. Thank you for your help--," he squinted at Crutchlow's ID, "Hans Heisenberg. You were most helpful."

Crutchlow let Fang leave the office before departing. Fernandez met him at the first intersection from the door. "Hey, how'd it go?"

"Dude, I thought you left me."

Fernandez grinned. "Nah, man. I didn't want that guy getting a good look at both our faces. Come on, let's get back."

As they exited a stairwell, the search party entered. "Stop! Identification!"

Crutchlow and Fernandez stepped out of the stairwell and presented their ID's. After a few seconds of examination, the guard held them back. In broken English, he said, "We're looking six people. Call security if you see anything."

"What happened to them?" Crutchlow asked.

The man shrugged. "We don't know." He looked further up the corridor.

"Well, okay, we'll let you know if we see anything."

The man nodded curtly, then motioned for his crew to move out. The search party disappeared into the stairwell, clomping boots faded away downward.

Thoroughly spooked, Crutchlow and Fernandez hustled to the quad with no further incidence. Having fooled Fang, they were confident they're infiltration was solid.

XIII

Hands still bound, Jackie and Lucy got stuffed in the bathroom as soon as Moreland and Crutchlow returned. Moreland set a cooked chicken breast on the sink wrapped in a paper towel. After a few days on a cereal diet, the Ministry of State Security agents practically ran into the lavatory, famished as they were. Keeping them on the edge made them more controllable, compliant, and weak. Considering their mutiny attempt, mercy wasn't on the docket anymore. He pulled the lavatory door shut.

Roberts and Fernandez sat on one bunk, while Moreland and Crutchlow sat on the opposite bunk. Perkins paced between, stroking his chin. "Alright, it's time to get down to business. We still don't have any clues about Chi-Hye. Now that we're all 'official,' we can focus on finding her." He turned back to the others askance. "Any thoughts?"

Fernandez raised his hand, face a grimace. "What if she's—dead? How will we get her body out?"

Perkins folded his arms, one hand stroking at his chin. "If it's practicable, we'll bring her home either way. That's next on our list of things to do. Find a way out of here. For when we're ready."

Roberts, elbows on his knees, looked up from the floor. "What about the Mossad guys? You think they might be undercover here somewhere? Would you recognize them?"

"Yeah," Perkins said, nodding. "I'd recognize 'em. As far as I know, that wasn't their mission. They just wanted Baader. As unprofessional as they were, they weren't incapable. It's a possibility they're hiding somewhere like us. I really thought the Mossad guys were supposed to be all bad-assed. Mossad guys back in the day. Whoo-boy, they were cold-blooded. It'd be nice if we had some more help. Especially with these two." He jabbed a thumb at the bathroom door. "Bottom line, though, they don't matter until we find Chi-Hye."

"We'll have to expect wounded," Crutchlow said, massaging his thighs. Muscles sore from too much stair running. "I gotta run more. I'm getting soft. Anyway, Chi-Hye, the Mossad guys—they may be prisoners and in bad shape, to boot."

"Crutch, Moreland, you two dig around," Perkins said, then eyeing Fernandez and Roberts, he continued, "and you two need jobs. So, Crutch, see if you can get them into something."

Crutchlow chewed on a cheek and nodded. An evil grin spread across his face. "Oh, I'll find 'em jobs alright."

Fernandez leaned back against the wall. "If we end up picking garbage, I'm turning you in."

"I wouldn't do that to you guys." The shit-eating grin on Crutchlow's face said otherwise.

"I'm warning you. I'll walk right up to the Don in charge here and point you out."

Crutchlow rolled his eyes. "Man, you're no fun. But okay, I'll keep you off trash duty."

"No toilet either."

Perkins resumed pacing. "We'll need some transport--."

The PA crackled to life. "Attention, attention. All Unit 57 personnel are to muster in the hangar at 0800. Attention, attention. All Unit 57 personnel are to muster in the hangar at 0800."

All eyes fell on Perkins. The spec ops veteran heaved a sigh and rubbed at the bridge of his nose. "Shit. Now what?"

"No worries, Perk," Crutchlow said, rising from the bunk bed. He tapped his badge with a finger. "We've got official IDs. We're on the roster. It should be just another check-box for us." He folded his arms, leaning a shoulder on the top bunk. "I've already got these two on the rolls. Just gotta assign them to the labor unit or something."

"Man," Fernandez said, "I don't wanna be doing some dirty job."

"Me neither," Roberts said, holding a fist toward Fernandez, who bumped it.

Crutchlow unfolded his arms and spread his hands. "Guys, I wouldn't make you clean toilets. I'll find you something." He stroked at his chin. "Something useful for our mission."

Perkins said, "The muster will be a good time to see everyone. The entire team gets to go this time. Alright, in the morning, we go to this muster. Get a good look at everybody." Turning to Crutchlow, he said, "You're sure these badges are good enough?"

"Hey," Crutchlow said, leaning off the bunk. "The head of security dude came in tonight at the last second. He didn't blink twice at our ID's."

Moreland held up a finger. "Neither did the search party."

Perkins clucked his tongue. "Someone needs to stay with these two." He glanced at the bathroom door.

Roberts shrugged. "We'll just tie 'em up good and tight with gags." He pointed at the bathroom door. "In there."

Perkins nodded and leaned in close. "Yeah, that should work. I don't like it much. They probably heard the announcement. Let's make sure we keep the muster on the down-low. I feel like that would give them an opportunity. You know, make it seem like we're not planning anything."

"We gonna liquidate 'em?" All eyes went to Roberts. He shrugged. "Just wondering. It's an option we haven't discussed."

"You're right, that's an option, but that's what separates us from the bad guys. We don't liquidate people--."

"Unless we have to," Moreland said.

Roberts licked his lips and leaned forward. "I'm just saying it should be something we'll have to think about. Let's get the thinking over now." He leaned back. "In case we need to DO."

"They're pretty small," Moreland said. "It won't take much. If anybody is squeamish about it, I'll take care of it if the time comes."

"Well, I wasn't saying I had a problem with it. I just wanted everybody to get it in the open. They've kinda become our pets. Hard to kill your pet."

Silence permeated the room.

Perkins gave a silence-breaking sniff. "Check. I'll put 'em down. I don't doubt any of you would either. So let's consider that base covered."

Relieved of the burden, all four said, "Roger that."

Nobody slept well that night. Fernandez and Roberts got the late watches. Crutchlow tossed and turned, while Moreland exacerbated things by snoring intermittently. A morning chime sounded at 0600 over the PA. They rose and made their way to the cafeteria. The odor of freshly made coffee wafted through the facility's hallways. After returning with food for their prisoners, Crutchlow and Moreland headed for the administration unit. They arrived at 0730 and found it empty.

"Do you think we'll look weird getting here early?" Moreland asked as they speed walked through the cubicles. The supervisor's darkened office loomed ahead. If they could manage it safely, Perkins wanted them to check-in again with Langley.

"I dunno," Crutchlow said as they ducked into the office. "Watch the door."

"Got it." Moreland leaned on the inside wall, peering toward the entrance. "If somebody comes in straight this way, they'll likely see us leaving this room."

"Well," Crutchlow said, pulling the phone drawer open and scooping up the receiver. "Think of something while I'm doing this." He waggled the handset and brought it to his ear. A reassuring dial tone hummed. The American started punching numbers.

Moreland watched the door intently. Every second stretched double. He glared over his shoulder. "You getting through?" He pressed against the wall and glanced at the door.

Crutchlow stood straight, gave a thumbs up, then set that hand on his hip, phone pressed against his ear, eyes scanning the walls.

"I got it. We'll tell 'em we're looking for Su because we wanted to report that dude last night. Fang." He glanced back at Crutchlow.

"Hi, just letting dad know we're fine." Crutchlow dropped the receiver back home and nudged the drawer shut with a knee. "We're good. Let's move out."

Already loitering in the walkway between cubicles, hands in his pockets, Crutchlow fell in beside Moreland. Near the entrance, they slowed to a normal walking pace. The door lock solenoid buzzed. Moreland grabbed Crutchlow's upper arm and pulled him aside into the cubicle farm. They crouched and scuttled a few rows back. "It's probably Long Su. We'll blend in after a few more people show up."

Moreland thumbed up as the chubby supervisor entered and waddled to her office.

"Let's move down by her office and see if she uses the phone," Crutchlow said in a stage whisper. They stole through the cubicles until they were directly across from the supervisor's office. Several minutes went by and all the supervisor did was shuffle papers and belch.

The door opened again. Half a dozen staffers came inside, chattering about the muster and missing people.

"That's our queue." Crutchlow said, pointing toward the people. They maneuvered to the door, quietly opened it and abruptly stood up, letting the door slam.

"Morning, Hanz."

"Howdy, Franz."

The pair made for their respective work centers. Before they got past the supervisor's office, Su stepped out into their path. The agents came to an abrupt halt.

"What's this I hear from the security supervisor about you two being up here after hours?"

Crutchlow and Moreland gulped in unison. There were too many people around to make this go away quietly. Moreland glanced at Crutchlow, who scowled at him. He turned to Su. "Ya, we ran into somebody else coming out last night. Since the door was open, we were just looking around."

"We're here to work, not to offer tours."

He looked at the floor. "I'm sorry. It won't happen again."

Hands on her hips, Su sighed, then said, "It was fortunate. Commander Fang was very pleased the department is so well staffed." She brushed between the pair, boobs rubbing against Crutchlow's arm, and clapped him on the shoulder. "You did a good job. I'll make sure it goes in your record." She headed for the door. Over her shoulder, she said, "Don't be late for the muster. I've got you two doing the tally."

Moreland let out the breath he'd been holding as the supervisor marched away.

Their eyes met. Crutchlow grinned. "Yes, ma'am."

"Damn, bro," Moreland said as they turned toward the door. "We'll be front and center for everybody to see."

Crutchlow heaved a sigh. "I know." He glanced at his watch. "We don't have much of a choice. There's no time for anything else. Let's make the best of it."

The two men bumped fists and left admin.

Dwarfed by the cavernous hangar, three hundred fifty personnel assembled in six evenly dressed rows. Chang Chen, Unit 57 commander, stood before them, hands clasped behind his back. Su marched up to him, saluted and fell in beside the commander. Crutchlow and

Moreland posted themselves by the first person in row one.

With a nod from Chen, Su stepped to a table, retrieving two clipboards with pens. She hustled to Crutchlow and Moreland, handing them pens and clipboards. Attached to each clipboard were several sheets of paper. A column of names ran down the left side. Crutchlow flipped through the pages, searching for their names. Moreland did the same. They confirmed the CIA team's names were present. Crutchlow made eye contact with Moreland and winked.

Chen, fluent in several languages, held mini-interviews with each person. It drug out a simple roll call interminably. Mandarin, Spanish, German, or English, Chen shifted from tongue to tongue effortlessly. Roberts used English. His non-conversational style made the interview short and sweet. Fernandez conversed in Spanish. He elicited a laugh from Chen in their exchange. Crutchlow half expected them to break out cigars. At this rate, it would be a couple of hours before muster completed.

Too paranoid to leave Jackie and Lucy alone, Perkins remained behind with the couple. Crutchlow would check his name off for the muster. With the entire facility in the hangar, the barracks area was so quiet you could hear a bed creak four doors down. Perkins sat on one bunk, suppressed pistol in his lap, with Jackie and Lucy sitting on the opposite bunk. The deafening silence amplified the awkwardness.

A slam up the hall brought Perkins to his feet, eyes on the door. He moved close, cracking it open. He didn't see anyone, but he heard hushed voices. A moment later, two men entered a quad three doors down. "Shit!" He spun on Jackie and Lucy. "Get up. Now! They're searching the barracks while everybody is out."

The pair rose, faces full of malice.

Perkins raised the gun to hip level. "Listen up. If either of you makes a sound, you're dead." He pointed at the door. "If those two get in our way, they're dead. If you don't want to die—don't want to see these guys die—you'd better do as I say. Understand?"

Jackie's eyes narrowed, but he nodded along with Lucy.

"Good." He returned to the door. "They're leaving a quad."

Perkins closed the door and turned back toward the MSS couple. "Here's what we're gonna do: when they go into the room next door, we're gonna sneak across the hall into a room they've already searched." He eyed the plenum above where all their gear lay hidden. He mentally crossed fingers they didn't look too hard, and swallowed, gesturing for them to get up and be ready. They complied without argument.

A few minutes later, they heard the quad next door open. Perkins nodded at the couple, directing them out first. Emerging right on Lucy's tail, Perkins pointed at a room two doors down and across the hall. They tiptoed past the guards, opened the door, and filed inside. He peered through the cracked door and observed the search party coming back into the hall and moving to their quad.

As with the previous searches, they snooped around the room for a minute before moving on to the next. Since theirs was the last room, the two men departed.

Dead silence returned. After a minute, Perkins felt confident they were alone and ushered Jackie and Lucy back across the hall and safely into their quad. Inside, back against the door, Perkins drew a deep breath, and let it out slowly.

After roll call, only two names remained unchecked. Yimu Fang strode up to Chen, didn't salute, and informed him that two of his people weren't present as they were on official business.

"What official business?" Chen asked, arching an eyebrow.

Fang leaned in close. "Prisoners captured after the plane explosion."

Within earshot, Moreland strained to hear.

Chen scowled. "Why haven't I heard about these prisoners? I've already reported they found nobody in the crash."

Eyeing the people gathered, Fang said, "I'm investigating the attack and believe I have several conspirators." He clasped hands behind his back. "They infiltrated the facility, and as we don't know if they have accomplices, I've kept their presence confidential."

"Where are they? I want to see them."

Fang shook his head. "I'm afraid that's not permitted."

Chen's face reddened. "What do you mean? I'm the facility commander."

"And I am a Ministry of State Security Officer."

The two men locked eyes, Chen seething at the rank pull. Though he was a senior officer in the Chinese Air Force, Fang could overrule him. No one defied an MSS Officer's dictate. Not even the commanding officer of a military base. They could protest and hold grudges, but opposing MSS personnel wasn't an option. A career ending violation and possibly his life.

Chen, fuming at the disrespect, straightened his olive drab uniform. "As you say, Officer Fang. However, do you not think it is important for a facility commander to be abreast of terrorists held in our midst?" He swept a hand toward the ranks.

Fang, inclining his head, said, "I apologize for the disrespect. With the loss of so many of my security team, I must be especially diligent. Secrecy is important right now."

Chen curled a corner of his mouth with a sniff. "Typical. Carry on, Officer Fang. Going forward, please let me know if the prisoner status changes. Or you find out about something nefarious."

Fang unclasped his hands, stood at attention, and said, "As you wish, commander." His response was loud enough for the crowd to hear. Chen acknowledged the gesture, throwing a halfhearted salute before spinning on a heel and marching back to his office.

XIV

A secret knock startled Perkins. They'd worked one out earlier. He never detected footsteps. Perkins moved swiftly to the door and cracked it open. Crutchlow and Moreland stared back.

"Open says us."

Perkins obliged, standing aside and holding the door. The pair filed into the quad.

"I think we've got a lead," Crutchlow said, plopping down on a bunk.

Moreland made for the bathroom. "There's a guy named Yimu Fang. He's head of security."

"Head of security?" Perkins asked, scratching his head.

"Yeah," Crutchlow said, "Chang Chen is in charge, but there's this Fang guy who isn't exactly part of the chain of command. He's the same one we helped last night verify some badges. They only got a skeleton crew for security now. Nowhere near enough to do the job properly."

Perkins nodded. "That explains how we've been able to run around here without much interference. Where are the security offices, anyway?"

Moreland exited the lavatory. "We haven't figured that part out yet." He reached behind himself and retrieved a folded document from a back pocket. "I did, however, clip these schematics today." He held the paper aloft and moved to a bunk, unfolding the document and spreading it on the mattress. The CIA team crowded around Moreland.

Jackie and Lucy were silent specters, lying tied up behind them on the other bunk.

They hemmed and hawed for a few minutes over the facility map. Nothing stood out as a brig or prison unit.

"From our surveillance," Moreland said as he tapped a finger on the schematic, "this building has got to be the security office." The square building he indicated stood in the hangar cavern. He leaned closer. "I don't see where they would keep several prisoners, though."

Perkins said, "That's where we'll start then." All faces turned to him. "Any suggestions?"

Fernandez said, "Why not break in after hours? Like we did with the admin unit."

"That's what I'm thinking," Roberts said.

Perkins turned from Roberts, eyes meeting Crutchlow's. "What do you think? Can we get in tonight?"

Crutchlow shook his head slowly. "There's no breaking in. A guard mans the front desk 24/7. I suppose we could take the guard out, but then someone might notice he's gone and--."

"That means we can get inside easily," Perkins said, hand extended, palm up. "One guy would be nothing for us."

"True," Crutchlow said, scratching at the back of his neck.

Perkins eyed Jackie and Lucy, who stared back defiantly. Lowering his voice, he huddled closer to the others. "Tonight, you and Moreland check it out." He turned to Roberts. "Me and you'll go check the body-barrels and make sure they haven't been noticed."

BAM BAM BAM!

Karl started from a deep sleep, scrambled into a corner, and cowered.

"Hey! Wake up! It's time for another interview." Muffled snickering disrupted Karl's terror.

My cell. I'm in the Chinese prison.

Something metal clacked. "Hurry!" The voice was louder. "Don't make us come in after you." More snickering. "You'll regret it."

I must act. Karl gathered himself, uncurling and sitting on the bed's edge. He rubbed his eyes, rose and stuck his feet into slippers. "I'm coming," he said, voice croaking as he shuffled to the door.

A pair of eyes watched him approach through the embedded small door hanging open. When he neared, the Asian glare on the other side disappeared from view.

Karl shook himself, limbering his legs and arms for a moment. *I'll only have a few seconds. Gotta get this right on the first try.* The specter of death felt close. A brief epiphany that these might be his last moments streamed through his mind. His heart thumped in his chest. *God help me.*

"Come on! Hurry! You're taking too long."

Karl drew a deep breath, pressed his lips together, and drove both forearms through the rectangular opening. A second later, hands on the other side tightly clutched them. Cold metal encircled both, followed by a stab of pain—Karl flinched. The hands let go and Karl withdrew them briskly. The little door slammed shut. Momentarily out of his captor's view, he slapped the injection site to his lips and sucked for all he was worth.

He spun while sucking and moved to the sink, where he spit the bitter chemical. Dark red saliva splattered on the stainless steel drain screen. He repeated, drawing out the sedative, glaring over his shoulder like a feral human, as if someone might challenge him for the meal.

The keypad buttons beeped the four number pattern.

Karl emptied his mouth, ran the water, and used the inside hem of his shirt to wipe his mouth. The door lock clicked. He dove onto the bed and pantomimed wooziness. His oral extraction hadn't removed all the drugs; a warmth spread throughout his system. So pretending to be drugged came easily, though for once, he was fully aware. The tingling in his tongue gave something to focus on.

"How much did you give him?" A man dressed in black fatigues groused as he pushed the door wide.

Another man peered around his shoulder. "I gave him the standard five Ccs."

They exchanged a glance.

The nearest one went to Karl's bedside. He banged the rack with a baton. "Get up. What's wrong with you?"

Karl sat up abruptly. *I'm overdoing it. Gotta remember–groggy, not unconscious.* He raised a tentative hand. "I'm okay. I'm--."

"Then get on your feet!" He stomped out of the cell, about facing to glare back at Karl.

"Okay. I'm going," Karl said, rising to his feet.

The guard scowled at him. "Shut the fuck up and move."

Karl shuffled through the doorway. Emerging into the corridor, he perceived how short it really was for once, compared to his foggy memory. *It seemed much— longer. I wonder what else I've misjudged. So far, so good with the sedative.* A shove from behind moved him along. They angled him to the right where a doorway opened to a stairwell.

The door blurred. Karl squinted, rubbing at his eyes, handcuffs jingling.

"Put your hands down."

The medicine-head sensation felt to Karl about like taking an antihistamine. *Easy pretending I'm sedated. They must administer a counter drug when I get there. Can't see how I'd talk much. Drool maybe. Damn, I hope I got enough out.*

Stairs led down. They ushered him downward. One floor down, the guards opened a door; they filed through—Karl sandwiched between. The corridor beyond was naked concrete. Light flicked on overhead, a single LED light on a skinny metal rod protruded through pipes and conduits running along the ceiling. Ten meters long, the corridor's end had doors on opposite sides.

The interrogation rooms.

Karl tensed, swallowing repeatedly, but he didn't resist.

Strength or not, I must try to escape. If I can find the others upstairs—if they even are upstairs—then I won't be just one. It's my only hope. I can do this. I can do this. I can do this.

XV

The CIA spy cell spent the next twenty-four hours gathering intel. Perkins, Roberts, and Fernandez watched Fang's movements closely. He went nowhere but his quarters, the mess hall, Chen's office, and the security offices. Crutchlow and Moreland scooped up the lion's share of information. Principally, the purpose of this complex.

Around the world, thousands of politicians, billionaires, oligarchs, and dictators stood ready for the 'Great Reset.' A theoretical endeavor to level the global playing field, dethrone the west, and strangle the world with control. All with a trans-humanist angle that sounded Orwellian despite the flowery rhetoric. Massive depopulation was a key component. Circumstances changed. Failure to release Bubonic hobbled the plan. Contingency plans were already in motion. The Ministry of State Security told Fang and Chen to remain on station until further notice.

An alternate scheme, developed in the event of a minimal outbreak, was ramping up propaganda pertaining to the virus. Social media mobs, mass media smear campaigns, and political ostracization revved up like an afterburner. Stoke the flames of fear all day, every day. Corporate heads and university deans, dollars signs in their eyes, declined to question CCP edicts publicly. They compromised themselves long ago. The proverbial frog in an ever heating pot of water. A foreign exchange student pays full tuition, providing lucrative students for the universities. The Chinese plan wasn't working perfectly, but it was still engendering the right global response of fear and panic. Fertile ground for emergency powers. The message would be clear: toe the line on pandemic procedures or risk killing millions and losing all that money. So the experts did as they were told.

Within the mountain complex, search parties looking for the missing staffers turned up nothing except some miscellaneous contraband, like shanks and heroin. The growing mystery was keeping Fang up at night more than the good-time girls. Commander Chen simply squatted on his haunches to await orders.

Crutchlow, eavesdropping from a cubicle, overheard Su tell Commander Chen one morning on the phone, 'It is better to wait and see. Given lack of direction.' She knew they had enough food, water, and fuel to last a year. The Chinese president would come through for them in the end. Or so the party faithful hoped. Would the world economy crash? Would there be war? As with most soldiers on the battlefield, they were clueless as to what was going on beyond their own surroundings.

The personnel in the facility, a broad swathe of disaffected humanity, knew something was up. When nothing happened after the plane crash and people started disappearing, they got suspicious. Lack of a security presence drew more concern. Few moved about the facility alone.

Moreland deflected any notice of their presence via his administrative position. Crutchlow gathered intel and helped Moreland. Life undercover in the complex became rather routine. Perkins and Roberts continued to make a body check periodically. Fernandez worked at infiltrating the Hispanic personnel's cliques. Because of the paranoid state of everybody's mind, he found it difficult. They mostly eyed him wearily and moved away.

Fernandez waited in the quad with Moreland and Crutchlow, standing by until Perkins and Roberts returned from their latest body check. At the barrel corral, a faint scent of death lingered, making the team nervous. Someone was bound to get suspicious. He rolled on his side, propping his head on an elbow. "Hey," he said, directing his call to Jackie and Lucy. "What's the deal?"

Jackie exchanged a glance with Lucy, who shrugged. Weakened from lack of food, and tied up, they had little fight left in them. Jackie looked up at Fernandez. "I do not understand."

"What's the deal with this place?" Fernandez asked, gesturing.

Jackie gazed at the bunk above, attempting to divine an answer there. Finally, he turned his head. "You won't like my answer, but I do not know. Even now, you know more about it than we do." He laid zip-tied hands on Lucy's. "We served for decades in Germany. This mission simple. Just two crickets minding their business. Require using only those the Government held in great trust because of secrecy." Jackie scratched at his head. "Keeping a secret requires loyal people, even in the most mundane occupations. So, we are truck drivers. Hauling supplies to base in middle of nowhere. Two years, we retire."

They both frowned and heaved a sigh.

Fernandez drummed his fingers on the mattress. "What'd you do in Germany?"

"They're MSS, Ministry of State Security agents. They're spies, like us. What's your freak'n real names?" Moreland asked from the lower bunk where he and Crutchlow lounged, playing a card game.

Chuckling, Jackie said, "We spied for China, of course." He ignored the name question.

"Of course," Fernandez said with a grin. "What'd you spy on?"

Lucy spoke up. "We ran legitimate business in Nuremberg. Did whatever MSS ask." She rubbed at her stomach, grimacing. "Please, we've finally shared something with you. May we have some food?"

Fernandez flicked his gaze from one to the other. He leaned over the side. "What do you guys think? Have they told us enough yet?"

"Hell no," Moreland said with a disgusted tossing of a card into the Rummy pile between him and Crutchlow.

"We really need to bathe too," said Lucy, tugging at her oily black hair.

"Now, that," Moreland said, "is something I wouldn't disagree with; you two stink."

"What else you got for us?" Fernandez said, settling back to his head on hand position.

Crutchlow picked up Moreland's discarded ten of hearts.

"Man, shit, I knew you'd pick it up," Moreland groused.

Grinning, Crutchlow said, "I've been waiting a long time for that card." He spread out a couple of sets and discarded his last card. "And that's game."

"Fuck!" Moreland said, throwing his cards at Crutchlow. "I ain't won a game against you yet." He rose from the bed, stretching and groaning. "Goddamn, I'm sick of being cooped up in this place."

"You and me both, brother," Fernandez said, lying back on the bed with hands laced under his head.

Perkins waited across the tarmac—obscured among parked truck trailers—while Roberts checked the body-barrels. A couple of minutes after leaving, Roberts trotted back. Perkins frowned; Roberts didn't have a smile or thumbs up.

"What is it?" Perkins asked.

Roberts, breathing heavy after his quick jog, said, "They're gone, and I mean all of them." He stared wistfully across the tarmac. "They were still here this morning. They must've shipped out this afternoon."

"Shit," Perkins said, thumping a fist against the nearest trailer. "But... must not have opened them or all hell would've broken loose." He shoved both hands in his pockets.

"Where did they go? I mean, how much time you think we got?"

Perkins shook his head. "I dunno." He peered around. "Where are we gonna hide any more bodies is the question?"

Roberts shrugged. "I'm sure we'll find somewhere to stuff 'em."

"Yeah." Perkins checked his watch. "Come on, let's take a spin past the security office."

"Roger that," Roberts said, falling in beside Perkins.

Far back from the hanger entrance, the security office was a nondescript, square, one-story building set back against the cavern wall. A single glass door centered at its front for public access with a small parking lot on the left, connected to a metal side door by a narrow walkway. The structure had no windows except for the front door.

As they strolled past, Perkins glanced through the glass door. He saw one person manning the front counter—like always. From their surveillance, they learned it was a 24/7 post, which made sense since this was basically the police department. There was never much activity in or around the place.

The pair about faced, retracing their trek past the security offices. "Alright," Perkins said, head swiveling. "Go peek in the door. I'm gonna stop and tie my boot."

"Check," Roberts said, breaking away. He approached out of the watchman's narrow field of view. Peering around the corner with one eye, he saw the guard slouching on a backed stool, playing a handheld video game. Roberts returned to Perkins. "Just one guy. He's dick'n with a video game."

Perkins sawed at his chin, eyeing the front door. "I'm thinking we should go inside for once," Perkins said, nodding slowly. He locked eyes with Roberts. "We gotta find something out. Too much time has gone by. Let's take it to the next level and talk to this dude." Perkin's eyes went to the door as he shrugged. "And see what happens."

Together, they strode up to the door. Roberts pulled the aluminum handle and held it for Perkins. The man at the desk lowered his gaming device under the counter. He straightened in his seat, elbows resting on the counter. Perkins smiled as he stepped up.

"*Gutentah. Spreaken zee doitch*?" Since the now deceased security goons were all German, he figured it wouldn't be a stretch if this guy spoke German.

Straight-faced, the man replied in Mandarin. "Mandarin or English."

Perkins gave a toothy grin, clapping Roberts on the shoulder reassuringly. "See Heinrich? I told you they'd be nice."

Roberts blinked, then fell into character upon remembering his cover name. "That's great—Winston."

The guard shifted on his stool, awaiting their inquiry.

Crutchlow and Moreland's access behind the scenes provided a complete list of everybody in the facility, including the chain of command. Confined to the quad, the team killed time reading over the names, memorizing those in charge. They plotted everything physically within the complex, using the schematics and taking walks around the underground maze of offices, workshops, and machinery rooms. Perkins knew who the important guys were. Including this no-so-important guy in front of him.

"Our work center supervisor has us helping with the search," Perkins said, glancing at Roberts. "Me and my friend were wondering where we should bring any info we find. Is this the right unit?" He lifted his hands. "Like if we catch a murderer or something." Perkins chuckled and elbowed Roberts, who joined in the chuckle.

The guard's eyes flicked between the CIA men, scowling and unimpressed. "Don't bring anyone here."

He raised an arm, pointing to his right and behind. "Use the side door. Ring the bell and someone will come." He folded his arms. "You don't belong in here." The guard glanced over a shoulder at a gray metal door five meters beyond the counter. "Now isn't a good time. There's an interrogation in progress."

Perkins studied the door, nodding. *Maybe. Just maybe.*

The guard returned his attention to the men across from him.

Roberts and Perkins made eye contact. After a moment, Perkins winked and nodded.

Turning back to the guard, Perkins shot out a left hand, grabbed the man's collar, and drew him closer. The man's eyes went wide, seeing Perkin's right fist coming at him. *CRUNCH* His head rocked back, and blood splattered from his nose. Roberts socked him too. The guard fell limp. Perkins let him go. He flopped down behind the counter, knocking over his stool. It clattered noisily.

Perkins leaped the counter.

Roberts checked the front door, then twisted the deadbolt locked.

"We're gonna need another graveyard," Perkins said as he took a grip on the guard's head and snapped his neck.

Roberts wrinkled his nose and leaped over the counter. Gawking at the corpse, he stooped and unclasped a key ring from the man's belt. A dozen keys later, they found the right one and opened the interrogation room door, finding a stairwell leading down, but not up.

Perkins hesitated on the landing, peering down over the railing.

"Whatcha think?" Roberts asked in a stage whisper, taking a gander behind at the glass door.

Perkins said, "Wait here. I'll check it out." He slipped down the concrete steps noiselessly. A minute later, he bound up the steps two at a time. "Goes down two levels. Didn't see anybody or hear anything." Without pause, he brushed past Roberts. "Come on. Let's get this body into the stairwell."

XVI

They guided Karl out of the stairwell. He paused, surprised it was only one floor down. A foyer area with a central corridor straight ahead. A single light on the ceiling midway cast a lonely field of light. *I'd been sure it was two floors. Maybe I'm going somewhere else?*

"Move it." The guard nudged him forward.

Karl snapped out of his pondering. There were only a few meters to go. He'd taken a single step when a commotion up the dimly lit hall drew all three men's attention. Flesh slapped against flesh. Two other guards wrestled with a man. The clutch of bodies tumbled to the floor.

"Ah, you bastards! Karl! Kevin! Somebody!"

Arnold! Karl's body tensed, and his heart revved up. Secretions of adrenaline trickled into his bloodstream. The fog of sedation lifted in a second. "Arnold!" Karl cried, lurching toward his comrade.

A stinging slap to his face stopped him in his tracks. He stumbled to the side a couple of steps, momentarily disoriented. One guard moved close to Karl.

The guard further from Karl said, "Secure Gruben."

Arnold, panting, grunting, screaming, legs flailing, clawed at the cell door's frame. "Karl! You better not give them anything. I'm not enduring this shit for nothing!" He howled in pain when a baton whacked his knuckles, breaking his grip. The guards might as well have been trying to put a mountain lion in a bath tub. They leaped over Arnold into the cell. One on each ankle, they hauled him inside the cell at the hallway's far end and quickly exited, slamming the door behind. The two men leaned against the wall, panting and checking scrapes.

Mouth agape, Karl's eyes met one of his guards. The man said, "Okay, go." He waggled his baton. As they led Karl, he stared at Arnold's interrogation room door. *Hang on, man. Hang on.*

"Here," a guard said as he stepped to a door opposite Arnold's.

Karl pressed his lips together. He reluctantly turned away from his friend's cell. The next thing his eyes settled on was a plain view of the cell's keypad. Confident their prisoner was too woozy, the guard flagrantly pecked out the entry code.

Karl saw the man's fingers make a zigzag pattern. Eyes wide, Karl lowered his gaze. *I got it! 2,4,6,8. Who do we appreciate?* He repeated the mantra in his head, terrified he would misremember it. *2,4,6,8. Who do we appreciate? I'd appreciate a hot shower and a decent meal.* The door lock unlatched with a solenoid *clack* and *buzz*, whereupon the guard grasped the handle and pulled it open. He regarded Karl with a scowl.

The man laid a hand on Karl's shoulder blade and pushed him along. Karl stumbled inside, feigning sedation. *2,4,6,8. Who do we appreciate?* Both guards fell in behind, guiding him to a wooden chair centered in the unlit room. Karl tensed, fearing a beating. Something to soften him up. Instead, he was roughly pulled back onto the chair where he plopped down,

119

hands restrained behind. Karl hung his head dazedly. Ever since they'd put the handcuffs on him, he had tried to keep his wrists turned their widest by pointing his thumbs outward, keeping the cuffs loose. *One more time! 2,4,6,8. Who do we appreciate? You, that's who!*

Satisfied he would stay sitting up and not slump over, the guards left. On their way out, they switched on a flashlight, laying it on the floor. The shadows began their dance on the wall in front of Karl. A few seconds later, the door slammed shut. Silence engulfed him.

The door slam was like a race gun for Karl. He immediately worked on the handcuffs. He held one side with the other hand, pulling with all his might. Metal dragged and pinched his knuckles. They were so close to falling off; he pulled even harder. After a few seconds, he stopped, letting out the breath he'd been holding. Chest heaving, Karl rose, spit on his wrist, then redoubled his efforts. The half freed hand kept giving until they parted. "Ha! I did it."

He didn't waste time admiring his accomplishment, diving for the flashlight a meter behind the chair. The handcuffs still attached to his left wrist clattered on the concrete as he clutched it with both hands. It was a heavy duty mag light. He showed the light beam on the door, as if it would fry anyone walking through. A few seconds passed and all he could hear was his own heavy breathing.

He ran the light around the room, establishing its dimensions and whether cameras were watching him. *A little late for that now. Should have stayed in the chair.*

Luckily, the room was entirely empty save for the chair and flashlight.

Feet shuffling and voices at the door.

Karl hustled back into the chair, dowsing the light. The room fell pitch black. He resettled into his seat and assumed the slumped position, body tense, ready to spring.

Click. Buzz.

Light from the hallway sliced into the room, widening as the door swung open. Voices spoke. "Get the other one sedated while I'm in here."

"Yes, Commander Fang."

Fang strode into the cell. "Your comrade has lost his mind. Where's the damned flashlight?" He probed in the dark with a foot. "Chi-Hye is feisty! Have you fucked her? I'm going to if you don't start talking."

The door slammed shut. In the pitch black, Fang never detected Karl's movements. Eyes adjusted to the darkness, he rose noiselessly. Karl's specter homed in on where Fang's head must be, swinging the flashlight as a club.

"And I'm going to shove this flashlight up someone's ass if I don--,"

Karl couldn't help let out a yell. "Aaaaah!" *CLACK*

Fang dropped instantly to the floor. Karl switched on the light and confirmed he'd been on target. Fang was still moving, then he was swatting for the flashlight. Karl jerked it away, but was too slow. Fang's hand hit it, knocking it from his grasp. It clattered to the floor, rolling to the wall, remaining lit. In full fight-or-flight mode, Karl fell on Fang, punching, elbowing, and wrestling. "Aaaaaah!"

XVII

Karl, a raging bull for the first few seconds, soon felt his strength wane. The initial blow he'd given the MSS Officer didn't take him down. Their struggle had reduced to a wrestling match. He was recovering by the second while Karl flagged. *So weak.... Can't fight him off.... I'm losing!*

Fang maneuvered, jerking Karl's coverall collar. Suddenly, Karl was on his back—Fang astride him.

"You piece of shit!" Fang slapped Karl on his right cheek. Heat and stinging pain radiated from his nose to his shoulder. "I'll teach you a lesson!" Fang had Karl's arms pinned under his knees. Flail as he might, Karl didn't have enough gas left to overpower his tormentor. Another slap from the left, followed by another from the right. Karl gulped for air, writhing under Fang.

Yelling outside. A fist pounded on the door. *BAM BAM BAM BAM*

Fang whirled on the noise, sweaty brow pinched in a furious scowl, face florid.

"Chi-Hye, you in there?" Came a muffled, familiar voice.

Karl raised his head and cocked an ear. *Perkins?*
BAM BAM BAM BAM

Fang returned his attention to Karl, abruptly leaping to his feet and backing toward the door. Karl rolled off his back and scurried to the rear wall. Back pressed into a corner, he met Fang's gaze. His countenance was a macabre shadow above the light. The security chief bore eyes on Karl. The Mossad man's face split into an evil grin. Fang narrowed his eyelids. "You're screwed, Fang. Perkins! The door code is 2,4--."

Fang lunged at Karl, who cowered against the wall, sliding down it.

"6, 8!"

Fang screamed, fingers curled like claws, spit flying. "How do you know the code?" He threw the flashlight aside, dropped to his knees, and gripped Karl's throat with both hands. "Guards! Guards!"

Karl tried pulling in air and got nothing, as if plastic wrap covered his mouth. He couldn't let out a sound either. He pummeled Fang with a flurry of weak blows. Fang shook him. The futile motions grew slower. Tunnel vision made the flashlight dimmer. A detached sensation came over Karl, like they were floating together in darkness.

BLAM The cell door smashed open.

Fang's grip left Karl's throat. He heaved a breath. A wild-eyed man in blue coveralls burst into the room, stiff-arming Fang to the wall above Karl and stabbing him a dozen times between two breaths. The assailant was like a sewing machine puncturing Fang a dozen times. Blood dripped and spattered on Karl, who scrambled from underneath.

Hands clutched his upper arm. He flinched and pulled away.

"Gruben," Perkins said. "It's okay. You're safe. We got you. Relax." Perkins took a knee beside Karl and looked away. "Go check the other cells. We definitely hit pay dirt." He turned back to Karl. "Hey, man, can you walk? Are you hurt badly?"

Karl looked from Perkins down to Fang. The MSS Officer lay gurgling in a growing puddle of blood at the blue coverall man's feet. Meeting his gaze, the man waggled his eyebrows, then about faced and exited the cell. Karl looked up at Perkin's concerned face and nodded. The CIA man rose, extending a hand. Karl clasped it and got hauled to his feet.

"You're sure you're not hurt?" Perkins said, looking Karl over, dusting him off. "I mean, you look more like shit than usual. Nice haircut, by the way. Very prison chic." His attempt to lighten things up fell flat when Karl didn't laugh or say anything.

Karl shuffled to the cell door, disbelieving it stood open. "Where are we? When are we?" He asked over his shoulder.

In the hall, Roberts was cleaning blood from his knife with a bed sheet. Perkins scratched at the back of his head. "Three days since the agency lost track of you."

Karl nodded, expressionless. He passed through into the corridor. Outside his cell, he gazed up and down the short passage. "What about the others?" Karl asked.

Perkins emerged into the corridor. "This all happened quick." He jogged to the stairwell, disappearing inside. A moment later, he reappeared. "We're still secure," he said, striding in like he owned the place.

Karl stood, disoriented, hugging himself. He turned toward the approaching CIA man, seeing him for the first time. "Perkins. It IS you. You American asshole." Karl's eyes cast downward. "I wanted to strangle you for bailing on us out there in the desert." He looked up into Perkin's face, hand outstretched. "Guess we're even now."

Perkins looked at Karl's shaky, dirty hand, then clasped it. "Yeah, well, good to see you, too," he said, smiling wryly. "What was going on in there?"

They ended the clasp, Karl folded his arms. "I had just tried overpowering our main tormentor, but it wasn't going well." He stared wistfully at his open cell.

"Impressive. You got more balls than I thought." Perkins clapped Karl on the shoulder.

"Anyway, Arnold's here, for sure," Karl said, glancing around. "I don't know about the others. They mentioned them, so I'm assuming they're here, too."

"Found her," Roberts cried from halfway down the hallway.

Karl and Perkins hustled down the corridor, halting at the door and peering inside. "Is she alright," Perkins asked as he entered the cell.

From inside, Karl heard Tonya say, "Oh my God, now they've sent Lare in to torture me? Larry Perkins of all people! Just kill me now!"

Karl grinned. *She's alive. What about the others?* He shuffled to the furthest cell that Roberts had just opened. All the cells opened with the same code.

Karl stepped inside. "Arnold? It's me, Karl."

Dark as it was, he couldn't make out more than a chair and body lying on the floor. Karl dropped to his knees beside his friend. "Arnold!" He grabbed Arnold's arm, rolling him over onto his back. "Arnold!" Dried blood covered Arnold's face. Karl shook him by the shoulders. Arnold's eyelids fluttered. "Speak to me."

"Karl?" Arnold croaked, peering through squinted eyes. "Why? How? They're jailing us together now? Oh, shit. They shaved you, too."

Karl smiled. "No. We're free." He glanced at the open door. "Well, we're free, but we're not out of this place yet." Karl leaned closer as Arnold rubbed his head. "You won't believe who rescued us."

Arnold glared at Karl.

Eyebrow cocked, Karl said, "Perkins."

Arnold snorted, then winced. "Figures. God does have a sense of humor. My aching head. Did he bring any cigaretts?"

Karl leaned back. "Can you stand?"

Arnold, rolling to one elbow, said, "Yeah, I think so." He got to all fours with Karl's help, then stood. "I'm starving. Are you hungry? I could eat the hind end of a hobbyhorse. And smoke a whole pack."

"Yes," Karl said, hand going to his abdomen. "Let's check on Kevin and Tonya, then we'll see about some food and smokes."

Arnold laid an arm across Karl's shoulder. Together, the orange clad Mossad agents ambled across the hall to the next open cell.

XVIII

They didn't find Kevin in one of the interrogation rooms. Karl spun away from the last empty cell, heart sinking. *He can't be... be dead.* The thought twisted his gut, so he pushed it out of his mind. "He must be somewhere else," Karl said, running a hand over his shaven head.

"There's another floor up one level. Looks just like this one." Perkins pointed at the ceiling.

Karl stiffened. *Of course, he must be upstairs.*

Perkins led the way up, with Roberts in the rear. Four doors mirrored the lower levels layout. Through a process of elimination, they determined which was Kevin's cell and opened it. Once again, the lock code was the same. Karl yanked open the second door on the right.

A phlegmy cough told them the young man wasn't well. Inside, they found a gaunt, pale Kevin Abercrombie lying face up on his thin bed. His curly hair was dark and sweaty, along with his orange jumpsuit. An unshaven face made him look like he'd aged ten years. They'd taken his eye patch. The empty socket was just skin.

Kneeling beside Kevin's rack, Karl laid a hand on Kevin's shoulder. "Aw, Kevin, what'd they do to you?" He gently shook him. "Kevin."

The fevered Mossad agent squirmed and moaned.

"He's got an infection," Tonya said, leaning over Karl, rubbing at her shaven head. "Bastards haven't given him anything for it. Lare, we got any antibiotics?" She turned and exited the room.

Karl shook him again. "Kevin, wake up. It's Karl."

Kevin's eyelid popped open, revealing a bloodshot blue eye. He sucked in a breath, weakly pushing away. "Mmmm, no…."

Taking Kevin's hands, Karl said, "Hey, hey, hey. Calm down. It's Karl. It's okay. We're free," He intoned, squeezing Kevin's hands.

"Karl?" Kevin asked, squinting, voice hoarse. "You made it off that plane. We saw it blow up." He closed his eye and rubbed his face.

The others leaned in over Karl's shoulder. He smiled down at Kevin. "Yes, brother, I made it off the plane. Are you sick? Did they… did they do something to you?" He glanced over his shoulder. "Someone get him some water." Perkins and Roberts exited the room.

"It started the day after they caught us. I came down with something." His brow furrowed. He looked Karl in the eyes. "I don't think they did anything to me like inject me with something. How long have we been here?"

Karl shook his head. "Three days. We're rescued, though. Perkins came back with help. But we're not out of the woods yet. You're ill and we're still trapped inside the mountain complex."

"Perkins?" Kevin laughed, which quickly devolved into hacking up a lung. The coughing fit waned. "I knew Asshole couldn't just leave the mission. What about Fang?"

Their eyes met, mutual acknowledgment of the suffering they'd endured.

"He's dead." Karl pressed his lips together, nodding. "One of Perkin's guys killed him."

Kevin frowned and nodded solemnly. "Good."

"Let me have a look at him," Arnold said, patting Karl on the shoulder. "Out of the way."

"Okay, okay." Karl rose from the bedside and turned to face Tonya, who was stepping back into the cell. She had lost weight, as they all did, and had a new haircut like everybody else, too. She still seemed full of spirit. No worse for wear. They wrapped arms around each other. He thought he would die here. That he would never see Gabriella or Tonya again. Guilt stung his conscience at the pain she must've endured. Karl broke the embrace, not meeting Tonya's eyes.

Perkins poked his head into the room. "Hey, I hate to cut the reunion short, but we've got some things to do."

Karl and Tonya faced him askance. He gestured to come hither with a finger. In the hallway, Karl, Tonya, Perkins, and Roberts formed a loose circle.

Perkins pointed at his companion. "This is Roberts."

Karl made eye contact with Roberts. "Thank you for ki—what you did in there. Honestly, I had him where I wanted him." He grinned sheepishly.

Roberts grinned. "Yeah, I could tell. Sorry I stole your thunder. Just another day on the job, though," he said with a bravado sniff. Karl held a hand out. Roberts shook it.

"Alright, we've got three other guys with us, but they're in the barracks. If we can--."

A confused expression creased Karl's face. "Wait. Where are we? Barracks? What's going on?"

Roberts and Perkins exchanged a glance.

Perkins faced Karl. "Okay, here's the quick and dirty. A few days after Chi-Hye didn't report in, they sent us out to find her. We found the portable jeep and the plane crash. After hijacking a truck, we infiltrated this place." He spread his hands.

Roberts said, "We still have the truck driver and his wife as prisoners."

Karl's eyebrows rose.

Perkins continued. "Once we got in here, we blended in thanks to the confusion from their entire security team dying in that plane crash." He looked at Karl, who nodded grimly. "Two of my guys work in the administration unit. The rest of us are officially unofficial."

Roberts showed Karl his ID badge. "Forgeries we made."

Karl's mouth fell agape.

Perkins nodded with a grin. "Nobody here has a clue. There's a weird, eclectic staff. Not many are Chinese."

Karl finally found his voice. "The plague! What about the plague! Is it real?"

Perkins scratched at a cheek. "Well, you took care of the big one. The other got sent to a place named Wuhan in refrigerated trucks."

Karl's eyes scanned the ceiling. "Is this a bio-weapons facility?"

Perkins folded his arms. "No. It's more of a bunker and internet troll farm. Fifty Cent army kind of stuff. And quarantine zone. It's all hidden in a mountainside."

Karl scowled. "Troll farm?"

"Yeah," Perkins said, "like they have hundreds of people who manage hundreds of fake accounts. They post and promote propaganda on Western social media. Been going on for years."

Karl ran a hand down his face. *My God. They captured us almost immediately while these guys break in and practically run the place.* He eyed Perkins. *He didn't say it, but I doubt they came looking for us Mossad people. Only Tonya.*

"Do we have a way out?"

"Yeah," Perkins said, unfolding his arms. "We gotta do some things quickly first." He faced Roberts. "Get the others, our gear, and the drivers."

Roberts nodded. "Roger that." He hustled up the stairs.

Perkins turned a slow circle. "Alright, I've got an idea." He sawed at his chin. "I think we can insinuate ourselves as the security unit. They're already short staffed and we can make any identification badge we need."

Karl knit his eyebrows and shook his head. "What? Are you serious? We need to get out of here."

Perkins locked eyes with Karl. He wasn't in terrible shape after captivity, but the mental toll was invisible. He surmised their Mossad training was adequate. "Yeah. Think about it. Whatever the Chi-comms are up to, we're in a perfect position to spy on it." He pointed a thumb over his shoulder. "We've even got a way to call home from inside this mountain."

"Can we use it? I mean, whatever it is, to call the Institute? Aren't you about to retire?"

Perkins patted the air. "In a minute. And don't remind me about retirement. First, we need to move our base of operations to here. This section isn't on the facility's schematics. We can keep Jackie and Lucy here more easily."

Karl cocked an eyebrow. "Jackie and Lucy?"

"That's the driver team we hijacked. It's been a pain in the ass, keeping them quiet and hidden. Like having life-sized hamsters. I'll fill you in later. Anyway, Chi-Hye, are you functional?"

A weary Tonya looked herself over. "Besides being hungry and tired, I'm operational."

Karl nodded. "Kevin is sick, but I think Arnold and I are good."

"Alright," Perkins said, stepping close. "Let's do this. Let's take this place over." He chopped a hand into the other.

"Wait, what?" Tonya said. "I need some food and a shower." She turned a circle. "Did you find a shower here?"

"There are showers in the barracks area."

She looked down at herself. "And some clothes. I doubt I'd fool anybody in these orange prison suits."

"True that," Perkins said with a smirk. "I've got a job for you, though. There's a dead guy upstairs. I want you to put on his uniform and man the front desk. Until we get moved in."

Tonya raspberried. "Well, damn, I was hoping for a little R&R. And it's just like a man to put a woman at a desk job. There's never any rest for the wicked."

Perkins rolled his eyes and heaved a sigh.

Tonya winked at Karl. "Like I'm his damned personal secretary or something." She then turned to Perkins. "Where's this body? It better not be all covered in blood and shit."

Perkins turned toward the stairwell. "Nah, his neck's broken. Might have peed himself, though. Come on, I'll show you and help get the clothes off."

"Ooo, that sounds fun. You really know how to show a girl a good time."

Karl turned back to Kevin's cell. "We need some food, water, and medication for Kevin. And cigarettes."

"We'll get it all," Perkins said as he pulled the door open. "Stay here for now. Tonya will be upstairs. It'll take us an hour to transfer everything and everybody."

Karl considered taking it upon himself to acquire medication. Instead, he nodded, then disappeared into Kevin's cell.

XIX

A few hours later, Kevin was resting with an intravenous drip of antibiotics. Moreland rustled them up from the medical unit, trading them for a Leatherman knife. Green Berets were competent field medics. The rest of the Mossad team got showered, fed, and dressed in fresh black fatigues. Lucy and Jackie took up residence in separate cells, the ones previously occupied by Karl and Tonya. They weren't happy about it, but their protests fell on deaf ears. By day's end, everyone had badges, except Kevin, who couldn't get up and walk to admin. They'd take care of it later.

With the CIA crew and gear moved, they gathered in the security office. After refusing to lay out of the meeting, Arnold helped him up the stairs so he could attend. Perkins took a central position. "Alright. Right now, we're safe. We've got a solid cover." He glanced at Kevin. "He'll be better soon. Until then, we maintain and gather all the intel we can."

Karl folded his arms. "We must get a message to the Institute as soon as possible."

"Yeah, we'll have to do that tonight. We've gotta let Langley know Chi-Hye is safe, too. After working hours, we can sneak in and use the phone. Do you have a secure number to call?"

Every Mossad member was used to memorizing things they couldn't write down. "Yes, of course. I just need an outside line."

A siren suddenly blared from the public address system speaker mounted on the ceiling.

All agents leaped to their feet.

"What the fuck is that?" Arnold asked, facing Perkins.

Perkins stared at the speaker. "I don't know. We haven't heard that one before."

"Guys!" Tonya cried. "Come look in the hangar. The doors are opening." She bound over the front counter and out the door.

They filed out the side door, jogging around front, where Chi-Hye watched anxiously. At the other end of the hangar, daylight sliced through the massive doors. They creaked and rattled as they spread ponderously. Distant roaring grew louder until an aircraft hove into view outside the opening. Three Vertical Take Off and Landing aircraft hovered outside, their propulsion systems set with thrusters blasting downward. The VTOLs waited patiently until the entrance was wide enough. They floated through the hangar in formation, engines blaring, landing in unison.

Hydraulic tail ramps lowered. Unarmed white Spock security androids clattered from the aircraft. They formed a perimeter within ten seconds. Each bipedal robot sentinel stood motionless. A man and woman marched from the center VTOL. The man stopped, hands going to hips. He gawked at the facility and personnel, obviously agitated.

Commander Chen burst out the Executive wing door thirty meters from the VTOLs. He hurried to the new arrivals, straightening his uniform as he went.

Still a hundred meters away, Perkins looked at the others while facility personnel quickly formed in military-type line-ups. "Come on. We should go to keep up appearances."

"Yeah," Karl said, breaking into a lope toward the strange meeting. Mossad and CIA agents followed.

In the world of cryptocurrency, one man's uncanny market instincts made him the wealthiest man alive. Iker Mar is one of the most recognizable faces on Earth. A college dropout twenty-five years ago, fast-forward a quarter century and he's a reclusive entrepreneur, renowned for hobnobbing with the rich and famous. TV interviews, YouTube videos, magazines, and books have all had his mug on them. And why not? He'd ushered in the age of digital currency. His secondary endeavor was an aircraft company aimed at making the first, practical flying car. The airborne vehicle pursuit naturally crossed over with robotics and AI. Android technology was something he never shared with the world. Keeping it for his private use. Terrified it of the consequences if it fell into the wrong hands.

The entrance Mar made couldn't have been more dazzling. As CIA and Mossad closed in on the android perimeter, a nearby Spock android's mirrored face zeroed in on them. A pair of skinny vertical hatches flicked open on its thighs. Handguns sprung out of the openings. Arms pivoted down, grasping an auto-pistol in each hand. Thigh doors slapped shut. Gun barrels stayed aimed at the ground.

Karl and Perkins froze.

"I don't think we should get any closer," Karl said, hands held placatingly for the robot's sake.

Perkins held his hands up. "I agree." He looked over his shoulder. "Everybody, hold up. Killer robots ahead."

It was about then that Karl scowled and squinted. *Is that—Iker Mar?*

"Holy shit!" Tonya squealed. "What's Iker Mar doing here?" She said, confirming Karl's recognition of the crypto-tycoon.

Karl turned back to her. "So, it is him." He panned his gaze across the bipedal androids in amazement. These were the most incredible machines he'd ever seen. They seemed completely autonomous and deadly.

Perkins and Karl exchanged a glance.

Both men shrugged and folded their arms to watch the exchange between Mar and Chen. The android phalanx surrounding Mar and his assistant, Julie Carrasco, permitted Chen through.

Arnold said, "Oh, shit."

Karl whirled on him. "You okay? What is it? You look like you've seen a ghost."

"I know the chick with Mar. She's ex-Mossad. We dated for a minute."

"Dammit, man!" Karl said with an incredulous scowl. "Is there nowhere in the world without some lover you've jilted?" He glared at the woman. "What is a Mossad agent doing as some billionaire's personal assistant?"

"Wait," Perkins said, holding the back of a hand to Karl's chest. "That's a good thing. Maybe they can get us out."

That gave Karl pause. "Come on, let's go talk to this guy." Karl marched forward.

"Hey, wait," an exasperated Perkins said, "the killer-robots." He shuffled a few steps after Karl.

"If he wanted people dead," Karl said over his shoulder, "we'd all be bleeding out right now."

The robots tensed, readied their weapons, but never brought them to bear as Karl passed between them, hands raised. Mar was berating Chen when he paused and watched the shaven headed man approaching in black fatigues.

"And who the hell is this? Patton, hold your fire."

A pale robot, red number one emblazoned on its forehead, stared Karl down with a blank chrome face. It holstered its weapon and faced away from the enlarging discussion. Karl and the others were on one side of the number one robot, opposite Mar and Chen. Ten more steps and they were standing a meter from the billionaire. Facility personnel kept their distance from the android cluster. They watched anxiously from their increasingly broken ranks.

"Okay, why are you in my subterranean facility?" Mar asked. Face flushed, he returned his glare to Chen. The robot-maker was tall with light brown hair kept closely cropped. For clothing, he wore black athletic shoes, blue jeans, a black Pulp Fiction t-shirt, and a thigh length black leather coat. No jewelry or flashy name brands save a wedding band.

Chen bowed, face creased with consternation. "As I was saying. The People's Republic of China has commandeered Unit 57 as part of emergency orders. Because of the pandemic."

"Pandemic?" Mar said, brow furrowing. "What the hell have you done?" He and Carrasco exchanged a glance. Carrasco's eyes then fell on Arnold.

"The hell they have," Karl spoke up. "They made the virus and released them on purpose."

"Arnold McGee?" Julie Carrasco asked, perplexed expression focused on Arnold.

"Oh, boy," Arnold said, dragging a hand down his face. "Here we go. Damn, and I look like shit."

The tall brunette dressed in khaki cargo pants and a pink Crypto-Kitty polo shirt stepped closer to Arnold, her hand reaching for his shoulder. She gently grasped his upper arm, a look of concern on her face. "Arnold? Arnold McGee, is that you?"

Arnold exhaled the breath he held and ran a hand over his stubbly scalp. "I'm—I'm—I dunno. Hi Julie. How have you been?"

Her head tilted. "Are you okay?" She ran her eyes up and down him. "You look like hell warmed over. What are you doing here?"

Commander Chen watched the exchange with narrowed eyes. He looked at Perkins. "Who are you? Where's Fang?"

Perkins ignored Chen, moving to intercept Carrasco. "Hey, we just rescued these guys. My names Perkins. CIA."

Chen stepped closer to Perkins. "I said identify yourselves." Agitated by his quickly slipping grasp on control, Chen said, "All of you, identify yourselves. I'm the commander here."

"Your entire security detail is gone," Perkins said, stabbing a finger at Chen. "It's over."

Chen's eyes darted between Mar, Perkins, and Karl. He knew there was nothing he could do to stop them. Unless he martyred himself. Chen straightened his back and adjusted his uniform. "Be that as it may, I am still responsible for the staff here."

Carrasco lifted an eyebrow at Perkins. "Rescued?" She knit her brows and looked Arnold over again. "What have you knuckleheads been up to?"

"It's a long story. We had an agent," Perkins pointed at Chi-Hye, who waved back with a cheery smile, "working with these guys. They went missing--."

"After he ditched us and had to come back," Arnold said.

Perkins gave Arnold the stink eye. "Anyway, we came looking for her and found them all held captive in this place. Do you think we could get a lift outta here?"

Carrasco blinked. "I—I guess." She turned to Mar.

Mar came closer. "You're CIA? What is the CIA doing in my subterranean facility? The National Security Advisor and Secretary of Defense know full well no one's allowed here."

Hands raised defensively, Perkins said, "Hey, we stumbled on this place just trying to find our missing agent." He scowled. "What do you mean 'your subterranean facility'?" Perkins jabbed an accusatory finger. "What are you doing here in Chinese territory?"

Mar's eyes flicked rapidly from face to face from under his brow. "I can't tell you everything." He lifted his gaze to take in the hangar. "They built it a long time ago. For a special purpose designed by my father. That special purpose is beyond top secret. It now looks like the Chinese went back on their promise never to activate it without permission."

"What are you talking about?" Karl asked, shaking his head.

Mar eyed Karl up and down. "Who are you?"

"Karl Gruben, Mossad. I and two other team members got captured. Not far from this place. Several days ago. They've been interrogating us ever since."

Mar abruptly pointed at the ceiling. "Christ, they even brought the reactor online. What the hell, what the hell?" Mar pinched the bridge of his nose. "Look, I don't know who's responsible, but I'm here to find out. Julie, I need the Chinese president on the horn--."

Approaching thunder of helicopters cut him off.

All eyes went to the hangar entrance. A hundred meters beyond the doors, five massive olive drab Russian Mi-26 helicopters lowered into view.

"Fuck me!" Mar said. "Now what?"

They landed. Several dozen troops spilled out and formed a phalanx around a man dressed in a dark business suit. Many gold rings on both hands glinted even from this distance. Dark Gucci sunglasses came off as he entered the hangar's gloom. While his guards moved in a tactical crouch, AKs at the ready, the man casually strolled along as if they weren't around him, heading straight for Mar and the others.

"Who is this guy?" Perkins asked. "Do we need to be worried?"

"No," Mar said over his shoulder as he moved toward the new arrival. "I know him. It's Malinov Antonovich."

The Mossad team and CIA operatives exchanged glances before following.

Antonovich's security phalanx parted with a flick of his wrist. As he approached, a grim visage didn't speak of something good. He and Mar stopped at one meter apart, facing each other. A moment passed. Antonovich burst into laughter. "Iker! You're part of this madness?"

Mar frowned. "No. Part of what? I just got here." The two embraced for a moment. They broke the embrace as Mar said, "We got an alarm that someone had used the outside line here. I had a feeling the Chi-comms were fucking around with the place. What do you know about it?"

Moreland and Crutchlow exchanged a glance. "Whoops," Crutchlow said with a shrug and half smile.

Antonovich looked past Mar. "Who are your friends?"

Mar peered around at the CIA and Mossad people. "You know, I can't really say." He turned back to Antonovich and shrugged. "They're not supposed to be here even more than the rest of these people."

"So you know about the Networks plan for a pandemic?" He waved a finger at the others. "They're not part of this?" The Network is a theoretical cabal of billionaire bankers who seek world domination.

Mar scowled. "No. I don't know about a Network pandemic. What the hell are you talking about? My sources have been telling me it's America, the EU, Russia, and the Chinese." He folded his arms. "So, you're saying this is a Network operation?"

Antonovich pursed his lips and clasped his hands behind his back. "Aw, well, they've done well keeping it a secret. They've been fooling around with bats and corona viruses for a long time. Somewhere along the way, they came up with a plan to spread a disease and 'reset' the world. I'd heard rumors, but not until we got some intel from mafia gangs claiming China tried recruiting them. We began an investigation, which turned up a pandemic scheme."

"That's insane. What crack are these Globalist dickheads smoking?"

"Fine quality crack, apparently. They're very rich." Antonovich gestured. "When I found out what they were going to do, I assembled a counter-terrorist company and came to stop them." He gazed at the surroundings. "Where are they keeping it?"

Perkins stepped forward. "You're too late. Gruben here destroyed part of the bio-weapon. The other part left for Wuhan a week ago. And there's an Italian connection we haven't figured out yet. Africa too."

Antonovich eyed Perkins. "And you are?"

"Perkins, CIA." He looked back at the others. "Me and four other operatives infiltrated this place a week ago."

"The CIA was on to this plot? Or in on it? I'd believe the latter before the former."

"Not exactly—."

Karl cut him off as he stepped closer. "We learned of the plot from an informant." Karl stuck out his hand. "Karl Gruben, Mossad. My team stumbled on this place in pursuit of a terrorist cell. We destroyed the Bubonic plague weapon the Chinese had weaponized and were transporting via aircraft to be spread worldwide. However, a different virus went on to a city named Wuhan."

Antonovich smirked at Mar. "Mossad here, too. What a party this is! How'd the Network let this happen? And here I left the vodka on my helicopter." He heaved a sigh and gave Karl's hand a quick shake. "Gentleman, something terrible has happened then. I believe divine providence brought us together at this moment. The unfortunate part is this salient point: a Chinese regiment of soldiers is making its way here. We flew over it two hours ago on the north-south corridor." He gestured toward the hangar doors. "I would estimate and hour before their here."

Perkins, doing the mental math, said, "We can't be here when they arrive. There isn't enough weaponry for--."

"We've got plenty of weaponry. My Spock androids are fearless, bullet resistant, and great shots." He grinned proudly.

"Comrade Mar." Antonovich spread his hands. "Do you really want to put that to a live test where you're in the middle?"

Mar surveyed the hangar with his eyes. "No. You're right. We need to leave, but not until they scram the reactor." He turned to android number one. "Patton, carry out operation Blown Light Bulb."

"Yes, sir." The robot about faced, breaking into a run. Four more androids joined it. They raced across the tarmac, disappearing through a doorway.

"As soon as they're done, we can leave. How many people are with you, anyway?" Mar turned to Karl.

"Nine."

Perkins said, "No, eleven."

Karl stared at him.

"We've got a couple of prisoners to bring back."

"Oh, right, the married team. We need to get them."

The pair of agents, trailed by their respective teams, jogged to the security office. Jackie and Lucy got led to the hangar by the CIA men. As they assembled to leave, the hangar lighting shut off. Sunlight glaring through the hangar doors doused the cavern in shadowed relief.

Mar glanced at a wrist device, pecked a button, and then looked at Karl. "Mission accomplished. They're on the way up."

Antonovich volunteered a lift if anyone needed it. Perkins, Chi-Hye, and the rest of the CIA team accepted his invitation, needing to return with their intel. The Russian would drop them off near Ulaanbaatar on his way back north. The Mossad members would go aboard Mar's VTOL.

Everybody hugged goodbye and gave thanks for the rescue. Karl and Tonya held their hug a little longer.

"So, you think you'll be back to Ulaanbaatar any time soon?" Tonya asked, twirling a lock of hair.

Karl heaved a sigh. "I do not know. The Institute will make a determination based on our intel and proceed from there."

Tonya chewed at the side of her mouth and nodded. The handsome Mossad agent had deftly shrugged her off.

Mar poked his head out the cockpit window. "Let's get in the air. We can wait for the strike team out there."

"Guess this is it," Tonya said as she grabbed both of Karl's hands. "I really like you, Mr. Gruben. Keep in touch, okay?"

Karl smiled. "I will."

Tonya scowled. "Promise?"

"Promise."

"Okay." She peeked over his shoulder. "Looks like your new friend is leaving. Better get aboard."

Karl pressed his lips together, nodded, then turned away. He climbed the rear loading ramp, waving goodbye one last time just before the ramp closed. She jogged away toward the hangar entrance and the helicopters.

Electric jet engines roared to life, and the VTOL shook. Inside, it was like a CEO's office. Plush leather

145

chairs, walnut trim everywhere, with a red Afghan carpet. They took seats and buckled up. It rose, rotated, then glided outside with the second one. The third aircraft remained inside, waiting for the sabotage team.

Antonovich, the CIA and his people returned to their helicopters, lifted off and departed the area.

Headphones on, Karl asked, "How do we have enough fuel?"

Mar smirked. "Because we use air for fuel."

Karl gave a puzzled expression.

"These are electric jet engines." Mar twirled a finger in the air. "They turn air into plasma. As long as we have battery, we have fuel."

Karl swallowed. "I'm guessing we have enough battery?"

"Plenty." Mar checked his watch. "Sit back and relax. It's gonna be a long trip home. And we have a lot to discuss."

The end of book 4, Operation Raven Rock

The Karl Gruben Spy Thriller Series:
1 – Operation Palmetto
2 – Operation Watchtower
3 – Operation Blue Eagle

Other Books By R.T. Breach:
Unity Pointe

rtbreach.com

Made in the USA
Columbia, SC
27 April 2023

15836809R00090